# Solitary Eyes on Fire and Other Stories

# SOLITARY EYES ON FIRE AND OTHER STORIES

John David Wells

# SOLITARY EYES ON FIRE AND OTHER STORIES

*iUniverse books may be ordered through booksellers or by contacting:*

*iUniverse*
*1663 Liberty Drive*
*Bloomington, IN 47403*
*www.iuniverse.com*
*1-800-Authors (1-800-288-4677)*

*Because of the dynamic nature of the Internet, any web addresses or links contained in this book may have changed since publication and may no longer be valid. The views expressed in this work are solely those of the author and do not necessarily reflect the views of the publisher, and the publisher hereby disclaims any responsibility for them.*

*Any people depicted in stock imagery provided by Getty Images are models, and such images are being used for illustrative purposes only.*
*Certain stock imagery © Getty Images.*

*ISBN: 978-1-5320-4460-1 (sc)*
*ISBN: 978-1-5320-4461-8 (e)*

*Print information available on the last page.*

*iUniverse rev. date: 03/08/2018*

# Contents

Maybe this planet is another planet's hell.

---Aldous Huxley

# A Zen-Like Cloud of Mystic Unknowing

Dean Erickson was drunk again, passing out. He had no idea where he was. Encased in a tomb of darkness, he tried mentally retracing the events of the evening, but he could not remember much of anything. There was nothing in his mind's eye but blurry images merging together, rolling backwards in his head, dissolving out of sight. *Did the cute redhead tell me she was too busy? Or was that last night?* He tried recalling a single event or person...maybe there was loud music in a crowded bar somewhere... someone tapping him on the shoulder as he was taking a leak...a mysterious woman who looked like Marlene Dietrich materializing under a foggy streetlamp...He tried swallowing, but his mouth tasted like a bowl of dust. Opening his eyes, he realized he was lying down somewhere. Across the room a dazzling beam of light sliced through an opening in a door like a golden knife, pulsating as if it was alive and breathing. Rising up from the floor, a dozen bloody meat cleavers swirled around the golden knife slashing brilliant red roses to smithereens. One of the meat cleavers stared at him suspiciously, roses tumbling from his mouth, rivulets of blood dripping from his protruding ice-blue eyeballs. He rolled over and grabbed something soft. At first, he thought it might be the red head, but it smelled funky, familiar. It smelled like his left arm; he was holding on to a pillow. Now, at least he knew where he was. In bed, passing out.

*Sometime in the middle of the night, a bestial fury roiled inside of him, bellowing up like an infuriated monster from the bowels of his stomach, snarling at the back of his throat. Terrified, he forced his mouth shut so it wouldn't escape. Karen appeared, lying naked on the bed mocking him, calling him a loser. Breathing fire and spitting sulfur, he began tying her up, handcuffing her wrists to the bedpost, stuffing a filthy sock in her mouth while slashing her face with poisonous fingernails, gouging her eyes out with his thumbs. He leaped on top of her like a ravenous wolverine, clawing and scratching her to death, skinning her alive as he bit off huge chunks of her tits. Her naked body wriggled like a hooked fish, eyes bugging out of her sockets, begging for her life as he stuck a blowtorch upside her head. For a few precious moments, he listened to the gentle comforting hiss of the gas escaping from the nozzle before squeezing the sparkler. Beautiful red-hot flames exploded as he twisted the dial searing every deceitful cell in her remorseless brain. He set the blowtorch down on the bed, lit a joint, sucked in a voluminous drag and blew a huge plume of smoke over her charred body and singed hair. Thin blue wisps mingling with sulfuric tendrils of smoke and ash swirling over her remains.*

Dean woke up, his head pounding from the nightmare and throbbing from a hair-burning hangover. Lying on his back, he stared mindlessly at blades of a ceiling fan spinning slowly around and around. He had no job, no wife, no kids, no place to go. He considered himself one of the luckiest men on the face of the earth.

Rolling over on his side, he detected a guttural sloshing noise deep within his stomach like vile liquid bubbling in a vat of sour buttermilk. He sat up, placing his hands on his knees looking down at the floor. Then he closed his eyes, massaging his temples with his fingertips before carefully touching his hair to make sure it really wasn't on fire. His head feeling unattached, lolling side-to-side like a woozy rag doll. If he could only get to the kitchen for a drink of water and some aspirin, he might feel better. Grabbing the bed post, he tried hauling himself up, but collapsed back on the bed following a roiling wave of nausea. Suddenly, the kitchen seemed a long way off. He looked up at the fan again. Abruptly, the telephone beside the bed rang loudly. He let it ring a few times before it stopped. He figured it was probably Karen trying to reach him again.

As hard as he tried, he could not remember many details about his marriage. It seemed every month he lost a year or two until now he could only recall sketchy fragments, withering bits of time, thin slices of random life…somewhere driving a car, turning his head, and noticing one of her silver hoop earrings…touching her red birthmark shaped like a strawberry…the fresh antiseptic smell of the bathroom after she showered…running to retrieve a rain-soaked newspaper lying on the lawn.

Dean realized they must have had a thousand conversations, but he could not recall anything they talked about, except one time she was upset that the neighbor's dog Brutus was tied up on the porch for a whole weekend in the hot sun. "Those fucking Collins' are assholes," she hissed. Something else came to mind. It was late; they were lying in bed together. She rolled over and said to the wall, "I think love is overrated."

Dean stared at his hands curled into vein-popping fists, constricted blood-red, clutching the sheet as if someone was sawing off one of his legs. He needed to calm down. He needed to get a grip. He needed to quit drinking. He needed these nightmares to stop. He needed to control his anger. He thought about the wisdom of Buddha: *You will not be punished for your anger, but punished* by *your anger.*

Lying motionless on the bed, he fought off the urge to pound the mattress with his fists. Instead, he said to himself, "Fuck it," and smiled ruefully, relaxing his grip, lifting his hands in the air, and then lobbed a couple of lazy boxing jabs to an imaginary opponent. Clutching his stomach, he rolled over to the side of the bed, choking and retching, afraid he was going to throw up. Then he forced himself up and leaned back on the headboard, trying to ease his wobbly, troubling mind. He wiped his sweaty brow with the sleeve of his shirt before grabbing the pillow next to him, and falling sideways into a fetal position. The softness of the pillow reminded him of Genie Madison, his first girlfriend. Closing his eyes, he drifted off once more..sliding back into the past…

*Slow dancing cheek-to-cheek in the gym, a golden mist bathing Genie's face in soft illumination…swaying and swooning…gliding effortlessly across the dance floor. Heavenly radiance flowing from her as if her soul was reaching out to embrace him….Hold me again, with all of your might…in the still of the night. And afterwards, alone together, moving closer to her, hoping the magic and mystery of it all would last forever. She smiled flirtatiously, kissed him gently and nestled her head on his shoulder. Her warm body silky soft, emitting the sweet fragrance of fresh lilacs and orange blossoms…*

Hours later, Dean sat naked in a cane chair in the middle of the living room listening to John Coltrane's *Love Supreme* on the record player. Holding a pencil lightly between two fingers, he channeled his Buddhist mode of intuitive thinking by focusing on a circle with a dot in the middle while trying to elevate his consciousness into a Zen-like cloud of mystic unknowing. God could be loved, but not thought—never known by concepts and ideas. Less thinking, more loving. He was not searching for a supreme being, but a cosmic revelation revealed from his third eye, the powerful extrasensory organ linking patterns and connections in everyday life. He was hoping to find some peace of mind by gaining inner-worldly intuitiveness in order to better understand and control emotions and thoughts, not only in other people, but himself. Most of all he was trying to control his anger.

The pale gray dot before his eyes slowly drifted outside the circle, dissolving into nothingness. The pencil hit the floor. Dean picked up the stopwatch lying between his legs. He clicked it: one minute and forty–five seconds. A personal best. Not up there with the Tibetan monks, he thought, but not bad. He put on his shorts, then walked over to the couch, plopped down in front of the TV and switched on an NBA game. It was in the third quarter and the Miami Heat was pummeling the Detroit Pistons by 22 points. Dwyane Wade drove the lane, sucked in the defense, then whipped a behind-the-back pass to Lebron James who promptly drained a wide-open three-pointer. Heat by 25. A few minutes later, Dean got up and went into the kitchen, grabbed a bottle of Seagram's VO and a liter of ginger ale from the pantry. He mixed a drink and then returned to the couch just as Lebron sank another 3-pointer. Suddenly, the phone rang.

"Hello."

"Dean?"

"Karen?"

"Yes, it's me. How are you?"

"I'm fine. How are you?"

"Look, I know I shouldn't be doing this, but I felt I needed to call you."

"Why?"

"Because I wanted to explain...I wanted to tell you what was—is— wrong with me."

"What is that?"

"I'm seeing someone...a therapist. She told me that I have a big problem...I'm addicted to sex."

Dean looked at the phone as if a tarantula was crawling out of it. Then he drained his drink. "You're gonna have to explain what you mean Karen. Addicted to sex? What the hell does that mean?"

"I have an abnormal sexual drive. My therapist...she thinks it is insatiable and I have an obsessive-compulsive disorder that drives me to commit immoral acts."

"Like cheating on your husband?"

"Yes, like that."

"Wait one second." Dean went back to the kitchen and retrieved the bottle of VO and ginger ale. He mixed a drink on the coffee table and took a healthy sip. "Okay, I'm back. Listen Karen, I don't know what to say. Are you apologizing?"

"Yes, I'm sorry I was such a terrible person...but I wanted you to know that I was out of control...I could not control my sexual appetites."

"And you are getting help for this?"

"Yes, I'm in therapy—and taking medications."

"To control your sex drive?"

"Yes, in a way."

"Karen, I'm a little confused. To be honest I don't think there is anything wrong with having a strong sex drive. It seems normal to me. You mean you have a disease like alcoholism?"

"Yes, that's a good way to put it. Some people can handle alcohol...but some people become addicted and lose control---"

"And make you want to fuck random men—and women?"

"I don't know what to say, Dean. I was out of control. I'm saying that I'm sorry for what I did to you."

"Well, no offense Karen, but it's a little late. I don't know what to say except that I am glad you got help and I guess your therapist knows what she is talking about---"

"Oh! she's a genius!"

"She must be if she can tell the difference between totally selfish behavior and a compulsive disorder."

"What do you mean?"

"Karen, you were only thinking about yourself—fulfilling your own desires. The sex drive is—well, it can go anywhere. I mean, you can't go around having sex with people while you are married---"

I know! I was wrong!"

"What about the lying and cheating part? Are you addicted to lying too?"

"I had to lie! I had to cover it up! Don't you see?"

Dean threw down another huge gulp. "Things fall apart pretty easy when they're held together by lies."

"What is that? One of your self-serving Buddha quotes?"

"No, it's the truth. It seems to me that your therapist is a quack. She's offering you an out—a way to escape responsibility for what you did."

"I knew you wouldn't understand. It was stupid to call."

"For Christ's sake, Karen, we were *married*. If you're single you can fuck five men or women a day and who gives a shit? I'm no psychiatrist, but it doesn't take Sigmund Freud to figure out that if you are going to get married you need to be monogamous—and that means channeling your sex drive towards one person---"

"But I tried!"

Dean polished off his drink, ran his fingers through his hair, and wiped his mouth with his sleeve. "So, what does this have to do with you being a lesbian and not telling me for seven years? Do you have an obsessive compulsion to sleep with other women?"

"Okay, Dean, cut the sarcasm. You know as well as I do that a person can't change his or her sexual preference---"

"Right. So, if you were born a lesbian, why did you marry me?"

"I was confused. I tried to deny my sexual feelings, but after a while I could not stop..."

"I'll say this much. You were a great actress—Academy Award stuff."

"I'm sorry about all the lies...I really am."

"That's okay. I'm glad you're getting help. You're right. I don't understand your actions—and I sure don't understand how you can be addicted to sex. You could say that about anything that gives you pleasure and you want to do again. What was I? Addicted to baseball?"

"Are you doing all right?"

"Sure. I'm okay."

"Can we still be friends?"

"Thanks for calling, Karen. I know it wasn't easy for you, but at least now I have some answers. Goodbye."

"Good night, Dean."

Dean glanced at the TV, watching the fans exit the stands following the Miami Heat blow out.

# The Prince of South Philly

Monica Clairemont sat in a battered moth-eaten wingback chair in the throes of a bad heroin situation. Her fevered sickness was further compounded by the wiry end of a broken spring poking her in the ass. Ordinarily, she wouldn't give a flying fuck about the stupid wire, but her grim junkie misery intensified every minor irritation in her life. The snake coiled in her stomach as her head lolled listlessly side-to-side like a drunken rag doll. Nauseous, choking and dry heaving, she grabbed her contorting face with both hands, opening her mouth wider to see if a mouse was crawling down her throat. The penetrating wire suddenly alive, pulsating, growing longer and sharper, piercing her ass like a gigantic hypodermic needle. She leaped out of the chair, landed awkwardly on the hardwood floor, and then curled into a fetal position.

Monica needed a fix, but her usual connections had dried up like her skin which was desiccated and bleached out like a parchment scroll scorching in the desert. Flicking loose flakes of dry skin off her elbow, she noticed a new purple abscess on the inside of her left forearm. She sat up on the floor, pinching the sore between her fingers, staring at the gooey puss squirting out, wondering why it was green. After wiping the sticky mess on the sleeve of her shirt, she glanced skittery-eyed across the room at her live-in boyfriend Joey to see if anything had changed in the last few minutes.

Nothing had. Joey was still vegetating, leaning to his left in a three-legged brown cloth La-Z-Boy propped up by a wooden box, mindlessly gnawing the rubber end of a number two pencil. His sagging, heavy-lidded raccoon eyes affecting a state of mind close to comatose. Monica focused her attention on Joey, wondering what had happened to him, the man who had been her dashing prince charming, her knight in shining armor. Her eyes drooped, lowering to half-mast thinking about the first time she met Joey...

"Joey, remember the night we met? Gosh, it was like…twenty years ago. We were slow dancing on *American Bandstand*. The song was "Twilight Time," by the Platters, and I said, "I hope I don't step on your toes." Do you remember? You asked me to go to the Chez Vous Ballroom to dance and listen to deejay Jerry Blavet's incredible motormouth monologues. He was the Geater with the heater, the Boss with the hot sauce! You were driving your hot blue Ford convertible, the one with the teardrop skirts and continental kit. You told me you were an amateur boxer and your ring name was Kid Kory. We cruised along the boulevard on top of the world, listening to Chuck Berry, my hair blowing madly in the wind. I looked over at you dressed to the nines in black striped shark skinned suit, and thin maroon tie, your arm nonchalantly resting on the steering wheel, a Pall Mall cigarette dangling from your lips like James Dean. Joey, my love, you were the scintillating essence of modern cool. We danced all night, remember? And when you took me home, you kissed me goodnight, whispering, 'You are so beautiful' in my ear. Remember?"

Monica lifted her tired eyes, glancing over at Joey once more.

"Joey?"

For a second she thought he might be dead.

"Joey!"

Stirring in his seat, Joey's eyes darted nervously around the room as if someone had knocked on a door somewhere.

"What?"

"Did you hear what I said?"

"Uh, no. Did you find a connection?"

"No, of course not. Forget it."

Now, the sight of Joey repulsed her. He was no longer that handsome, dark-haired Italian lover that all the girls swooned over. All the drugs, physical abuse, and junk-craving agitation seemed to have shrunken his gloomy face to the size of a potato.

"Did you call Sal?" asked Joey, chomping on the pencil, then spitting out bits of eraser.

"You asked me that five minutes ago."

"And?"

"Christ, Joey! I told you he doesn't have any fuckin' dope! Nobody in this fuckin' town has any dope! For all I know, the whole world just ran out of all the fuckin' heroin in the fuckin' world!"

"Okay… chill. What about the Prophet?"

Monica squirmed on the floor as if she had a splinter in her ass. "Oh *great,* Joey. Yeah, call the Prophet. I'm sure the guards at Rahway would let you into his cell to score some Peruvian White."

"He's in jail?"

"Just thirty years."

"Shit. We're screwed."

The snake roiling inside Monica, hungry for a blast, reminding her that he was going to get real nasty. She was already showing signs of low-grade flu symptoms, heading for convulsions, thinking, *I'm not gonna have a monkey on my back; it's gonna be a fuckin' gorilla. King-motherfucking-Kong is gonna come pounding down my door any minute!*

She looked at Joey again. Her husband was now Mr. Potato Head holding the pencil up to his face, peering at it cross-eyed, as if the shredded ends held clues to a mysteries of the universe. His face squeezed tight, lips pursed, while his eyebrows narrowed to a thin black line. He looked like a hobo who just lost a dollar in a Coke machine.

Monica knew the odds of Joey doing anything practical like getting a job, buying groceries, or cleaning the apartment was beyond the scope of any known arithmetic probability. He was useless; but then again, so was she. Isolated and alone together for so long, they were like two sick prisoners sharing the same cell. Monica gazed around the room, trying to find something more stimulating than watching Joey chew up a pencil. The living room was sparsely furnished with the help of the Salvation Army. No pictures, curtains, or flowers to brighten the surroundings, and the lone window in the center of the room was shut tight despite the oppressive heat. A yellowed vinyl shade allowed a few splinters of light to penetrate the edges. As her withdrawal exacerbated, Monica's body oscillated between extreme overheating and shivering cold sweats. At the moment, she felt like an embalmed mummy roasting in a blast furnace.

"Monica."

"What?"

"We're out of cigarettes."

"No shit, Joey. We're out of everything."

"Any big butts in that ashtray?"

"No."

"Maybe it's a good time to quit."

"Joey, it's not a good time to quit anything."

Joey turned on a harsh floor lamp, illuminating sharp, austere lines on his face. From this angle he appeared sculpted in granite, gray and inanimate like a miniature Mt. Rushmore figure.

Monica crawled back into the wingback chair, and began considering her options. It did not take her long to figure out that she was down to one: her brother Danny. *He would know what to do. Danny would keep the snake at bay and King Kong away from the door.* Abruptly, she stood up, grabbed her pocketbook, and walked past Joey who was writing in a small notebook.

"I'll be back. I'm gonna make a call."

"You got a connection?"

"No, I'm calling my brother."

"He doesn't have any dope."

"He's got as much as you have."

Monica opened the front door and trotted down the stairs to a corner phone booth resembling the last structure standing in a war zone. Most of the glass was busted out and shattered with random pieces held together by spidery webs of chicken wire. The folding door was half-way rusted shut, allowing Monica with just enough space to squeeze through the narrow opening. The phone book had long since been ripped out, and the phone itself was a marvel of modern urban street art, adorned with crude carvings of nude women, cock and balls, and scratchy phone numbers. The phone would have been destroyed long ago, but the drug dealers needed it for their 24/7 operations. Monica lifted the receiver, dropped a quarter in the slot, and dialed Danny's number in Palmyra, New Jersey.

Danny's wife, Karen answered the phone.

"Hello."

"Oh hi, Karen. This is Monica.. Is Danny home?"

Monica detecting a deliberate pause. "Yes. Just one minute."

Surveying the raunchy graffiti, her eyes landed on "Mary Ann Loves to Suck Big Black Dicks."

"Hello," said Danny.

"Oh Danny! This is Monica. I need you to come and get me. Joey is beating me up and trying to pimp me out! I need to get out of here *now!*"

Danny audibly sighed, rolling his eyes towards the ceiling. "Where are you? Who's Joey?"

"Joey Corelli! He's my worthless junkie boyfriend! You don't remember him?"

"Why should I?"

"He was that gorgeous hunk I dated from *American Bandstand.*"

"The boxer?"

"Yes! I ran into him four months ago, and we've been living together."

"And now he's beating *you* up?"

"Yes!"

"Monica, the only time you ever call me is when you need something."

"That's not true! Look, Danny, I'm in North Philly. You've got to help me! He's dangerous!"

"Christ Monica, it's one o'clock in the fucking morning. I've got like… a wife… two kids… stuff like that."

"He's crazy! He's got a knife!"

Danny held the receiver away from his ear. Glancing over at Karen, he tilted the phone in her direction, shrugging his shoulders.

"Okay, what's the address?"

"234 Parish Street. Hurry! I'm afraid to go inside, so I'll be waiting on the steps."

"I'll be there within the hour. Don't go inside."


Danny left the house and drove over the Teconey-Palmyra Bridge spanning the Delaware River. He parked the car and walked towards the row house. As he rounded a corner, he spotted Monica on top of the steps screaming at Joey who was standing in the open doorway.

"You cowardly bastard! Hitting a defenseless woman! I'm getting out of here and never coming back!"

Joey leaned back, throwing his arms up defensively. "What the hell are you talking abo—"

"Danny! Thank God! Get me out of here!"

Monica ran down the street, pausing at the corner, unsure where the car was parked. Danny spun around, quickly followed her, then grabbed her by the arm and took her to the car. They both jumped in, Danny slamming down on the accelerator, speeding and fishtailing down the street as if they were bank robbers in a getaway car.

"Are you okay?" asked Danny, running a red light before swerving around a corner.

"Thank God you came when you did! He was going to kill me!"

"Really? He didn't look like he was going to kill anybody."

"Don't let that fool you. He beat me plenty of times."

Danny eased up on the gas, resuming normal speed. "So, Monica, where we going?"

"Can I stay at your place tonight? Just for one night? I can sleep on the couch. I won't bother anybody."

"Monica, where are you going to live?"

"Listen, Danny, you need to help me! I need some money real bad! I'm withdrawing, and I need a fix—real bad! You have no idea how sick I am!"

"So this is what it's all about—you scoring dope."

"No, I swear! I'm going on a methadone program tomorrow—but I need a fix tonight!"

"No way, Monica. You're coming to my house. You can make it through the night. I've got some Xanax at my place. I'll get you to a detox center tomorrow morning."

"You don't understand! I'm sick! I need something right now!"

"Sorry, but I'm not driving around the hood looking for a bag of dope. You'll get us killed."

"Do you have any money?"

"Jesus Christ! No, I do not have any money for your stupid heroin habit. Now just shut the fuck up! You're getting on my nerves."

Monica leaned back in the seat, remaining silent until they neared Danny's house. She made one last effort.

"Listen, Danny, I know a guy right around here. He's cool! Just let me see if he's holding, okay?"

"No, Monica, it's after two in the morning."

"Okay, but you got Xanax, right?"

"Just a couple, but you can have them—then you're going to bed."

In the morning Danny looked in on his sister. She was still in her room. He helped Karen get the kids off to school and then left for work at eight o'clock. He returned at five-thirty. This time Monica was not in the bedroom. He checked with Karen and the boys. They had not seen her all day. Danny had no idea where she might be. She had no fixed address or telephone number. He picked up the phone and called his brother Jackie.

"Hey, Jackie. Monica's missing again."

"You saw her?"

"She was in Philly with some scumbag. I brought her home last night. I came back from work and she was gone. She could be anywhere."

"She has no car, no money, no dope, and no job, right?"

"That's about it."

"Pick me up in a half-hour."

"You got an idea?"

"Well, let's narrow it down. She's either in jail, at the hospital, or at the Center, right?"

"I guess that about covers it."

"So let's go to the most obvious."

"Right. See you in a few."


The Center was the sleaziest part of Camden, New Jersey, just across the Delaware River from Philadelphia. No one was sure how it got its name, but these days it was the center of crime, drug dealing, prostitution, strip joints, sex shops, and X-rated video stores. It was a hustling netherworld of hookers, petty criminals, dealers, runners, touts, stick-up artists, crankheads, crackheads, pipeheads, and junkies. Danny and Jackie cruised several blocks, passing broken-down row houses, boarded-up businesses, liquor stores touting lottery tickets, and a mini-mart run by two Yemeni brothers. A steady stream of barking doormen clad in cheap polyester suits and loud ties exhorted them to come in and sample their topless dancers while high-heeled, grease-painted streetwalkers hollered out to the guys, offering the promise and allure of sexual paradise. Slouching, bling-draped pimps in wide-brimmed hats drove methodically along the avenue, passing by in sleek, tinted black sedans, searching for the suckers, the horny, the fiends, the wretched, and the desperate.

They stopped at a red light. Out of nowhere, a brazen hooker ran up to the car wearing clown-inspired makeup, and decked out in a black leotard, purple high heels, red mini-shorts, and a bright yellow Dolly Parton wig. She propped her elbows on the car and leaned in towards Jackie, her carnival face filling up the entire passenger-side window.

"Hey, sweeties! You guys looking for a real good time?"

"No," Jackie stammered, "We're… just looking."

"Come on," she moaned. "Blow job for fifty—and that's a real bargain."

The light changed. Danny took off, sending the prostitute reeling backwards, her arms flailing wildly, struggling to keep her balance. Jackie turned around in time to see her giving them a murderous look and the finger.

Cruising past a neon-lit Chinese restaurant squeezed between a tattoo parlor and a leather sex shop, they spotted three haggard old black women crammed together on a row house stoop with nothing to do but witness the neighborhood swirling down a toilet bowl.

Danny and Jackie slowed for a red light. A skinny black kid rushed up to them sporting a Chicago White Sox baseball cap and a billowing white T-shirt. He banged on Jackie's window. "Hey, guys, whaddaya want? Coke? Pot? Pussy? Crank?"

Jackie, rolled down the window a few inches. "No, pal, we're just looking. Thanks anyway."

"You don't want no pussy, man?"

The light changed, Danny gunned the engine.

"This is her element," said Danny.

"Right. Her element."

The two brothers finally located their sister staggering out of a dive bar on Broadway, lost, strung out, and barely able to stay upright.

"Jesus," said Jackie. "She looks like the bride of Frankenstein on meth."

Danny pulled up beside her. "Hey, Monica! Get the fuck in here!"

"Danny? Jackie? What are you guys doing here? Did you bring me anything? I'm dying!"

"No, Monica," said Jackie, a pair of opaque eyes peering at him from inside two skeletal black holes. "We didn't bring you anything. We're taking you to a hospital. Get in."

Monica was at the end of the line and without any motivation to move in any other direction. She slid into the backseat, contorting and twisting her face as if she was locked in a colonial pillory. Her naturally curly wheat-colored hair was a mass of sweaty gnarls and tangles sticking to the sides of her face, her body shivering as both hands gripped the backseat, knuckles turning white from lack of blood.

"Guys, I'm really sick."

Danny glared at her. "I know. That's why we're taking you to a hospital."

They drove her to a hospital in the town of Haddonfield. Following a series of interviews and filling out numerous forms, she was finally admitted. Her brothers left her in the care of the hospital.

Two days later, Monica was languishing in the hospital bed, sick, throwing up, and convulsing from withdrawal. Delirious and hallucinating, she swore an army of tiny crabs were crawling under her skin, trying to claw their way out. An obese bi-polar woman with greasy hair and rippling rolls of fat bulging out of her gown was lying next to her, vacillating between bouts of corpse-like inaction, and relentless nervous agitations In her manic stage, she could run her mouth for hours. During one of her incessant blathering sessions, the fat lady discovered that Monica dated the legendary Joey Corelli.

Gushing like a school girl, she burned Monica's ears, going on and on about Joey Corelli, "Did you know he was the absolute *Prince* of South Philly? Oh! Yes! Kid Kory! You went out that dynamite superstar who hung out with the coolest, hippest people on South Street? I heard he was friends with Joe DiMaggio and Marilyn, and he knew Steve McQueen, and taught Muhammad Ali how to box." Eyeing Monica suspiciously, she found it hard to believe this wasted junkie puking all over herself actually dated the great Joey Corelli. "You really hooked up with Kid Kory? Definitely, the hippest guy—ever! Did you know he was the first one in Philadelphia to wear black socks and sandals?"

15

Monica turned her back to the woman, her haunted, smudge-pot eyes staring blankly at the adjacent wall, hoping she would shut the fuck up. She folded her arms over her head, squeezed the pillow into her face, and closed her eyes. In spite of the woman's non-stop twaddle and her own gnawing anguish, Monica floated briefly into a languorous daydream, trying to remember if Joey Corelli had worn black socks and sandals the night they went dancing at the Chez Vous Ballroom.

# A Bony-Headed Psychopath

Betty Kincade was a widower with three kids who married Roy Shifflette after knowing him for only three months. No one in her family could figure out what Betty saw in Roy Shifflette. To everyone who knew him Roy was a slack-jawed, bony-headed psychopath. But, Roy put on a good act in the beginning, keeping his previous life a secret, especially the two years he served in jail for savagely beating up his ex-wife Mildred. Roy told Betty that Mildred was a low-down whore who ran off with the town sheriff. Mildred did not exactly run off; she divorced Roy while he was in jail.

Roy bought a row house in the middle of the black section of Baltimore with the insurance money Betty got from her deceased husband. Things might have worked out, but Roy was a ignorant jackass who hated black people. After landing a job at the Bethlehem Steel plant in Sparrows Point, he told everybody he was a "structural steel detailer," but in reality he was a spot welder in a machine shop adjacent to the main industrial complex. Roy hated the job and all his coworkers. "Too many goddamn Yankees and ball busters," was the way he described them. The feelings were mutual. Roy's fellow employees considered him one of the biggest assholes on the planet. They never called him by his first name; he was always "that Shifflette asshole" or "the Twerp."

The Civil War was very much on Roy's mind having traced his ancestry back to John Brown, the fanatical abolitionist. Roy claimed John Brown was his great-great-grandfather. This was not true, although his mother did own John Brown's sword and rifle, stolen by a ne'er-do-well distant uncle at Brown's hanging in Harpers Ferry, West Virginia. Roy prided himself on his Rebel heritage, still carrying a grudge for having lost the war to the "fuckin' Federals." Roy heard stories about John Brown's malevolent, demonic personality, and was doing his best to continue the family tradition. Roy attributed his sudden, sadistic rages to his infamous bloodline and in drunken monologues bellowed blustery exclamations like, "John Brown's body may be molding in his grave, but I'm alive and ready to kick some ass!" Unfortunately, the ones who got their asses kicked were his wife and three step-kids.

Dinner time in early November. Roy holding court at the head of the table with one hand gripping a can of beer and the other holding a fried chicken leg in the air. The sides of the beer can and chicken leg stained from Roy's blackened oily hands, droplets of grease dripping on his oleaginous work shirt. He rubbed his shirt with the chicken leg still in his hand, bit off a chunk, and then guzzled it down with a sloppy slug of beer, a circle of foam rimming his mouth.

Two boys, Billy and Robbie were eating quietly next to Roy, their bodies stiff, heads bent down, staring at their food. Betty and step-daughter Ginny sat across from him. Betty slumping forward as if any second she might fold over into her food.

Roy always insisted that the children eat everything on their plates. His logic was never entirely clear, but it usually involved comparing the kids' lucky lives to emaciated people starving in third-world countries, surviving on earthworms and tree bark. The oldest sibling Ginny hated peas. She glowered at the peas on her plate as if *they* were a pile of earthworms. Just the thought of shoving those slimy green morsels in her mouth made her stomach recoil and roll over. She was determined to avoid ingesting those tiny little bastards.

When Roy was not looking she scooped a spoonful peas, carefully wrapping them in a napkin under the table. Then she leveled the mound of peas, forming single rows, trying to give Roy the impression there were not enough peas to form a whole pile. Monica was confident her ploy would work since her step-father was already dip-shit drunk, slobbering over his own pile of peas. "So," said Roy, licking his motor oil fingers. "What did you do at school today?"

The three kids glanced furtively at each other, pulses quickening, not sure who he was asking. Ginny being the oldest, offered an answer.

"Oh, nothing much. We had a contest to see who could name all the capitals of the United States."

"Is that it?" demanded Roy, suddenly more alert, his elbows propped on the table, a knife in one hand, a fork in the other. "What about dinner etiquette? They teach you how to behave at the dinner table in that fancy school?"

"Now, Roy," said Betty patiently, "Let's not start something."

Without warning, Roy leaped over the table like a bloodthirsty wolverine, grabbing Monica by the neck with both hands, slapping her face back and forth like a rag doll before slamming her viciously back in the chair. As she hit the chair, it collapsed beneath her, sending her sprawling on the floor.

Roy stood over Monica, thrusting his fists into the air like a triumphant boxer, as she cowered on the floor coiled in a fetal position, her body shaking violent spasms.

"You stupid little bitch! You think I'm stupid? I saw what you did! Now here's the rest of your peas! Eat them!"

Roy hurled a bowl of peas in Monica's face, splashing her with a mass of wet green slop. Danny and Jackie rushed to her defense, but Roy pushed them aside, whacking Danny in the head, shoving Jackie into a corner. Jackie hit the floor, banging his head against the wall, a steak knife lying inches away. He was about to reach for it, but Roy glared at him, screaming, "Jackie, go to your room!"

"Me? What did I ?"

Roy reached down, grabbed Jackie by the shirt collar, slapping him in the face.

"Roy!"cried Betty."Are you out of your mind?"

She ran up to him, kicking his legs, thumping her fists on his chest. An evil grin spread across Roy's face before hit her over the head with the empty bowl of peas. Betty crashed into the table like a sack of potatoes, rolling over and landing on the floor, food and tableware flying all over the kitchen.

"You're all a bunch of fuckin' idiots, ya hear! You think I don't know what's going on around here? You're all making fun of me behind my back, mocking me like a retard! Well, I'm not going to stand for it! Not in my house!"

Roy grabbed his cooler, marched into the living room, sunk down in his easy chair and turned on the TV.

The kitchen resembled a war zone. Betty and the kids gathered themselves, surveyed the wreckage, and checked their physical condition. No one was seriously hurt, but Betty had an ugly bruise forming on her forehead. Monica's face and neck were still flushing red and purple blotches. No one said a word as they began putting the disheveled kitchen back together.

Monica finally spoke, uttering in a low, determined voice, "I don't care. I still hate peas."

The next day Roy decided to clean out the rats from the basement of the house. He marched into the boys' room, shaking Danny and Jackie awake, ordering them to pick up the empty beer cans in the living room.

"After you knuckleheads finish, we're taking care of those rats in the cellar."

Danny and Jackie were still rubbing the sleep from their eyes. Danny was sitting on the lower bunk bed, searching for some pants to put on. In the upper bunk, Jackie rolled over, covering his head with a blanket.

"What do you mean... about those rats?" asked Danny.

"We gotta clear 'em out. You don't want rats running into your room at night, do you?"

As usual, Roy made the boys' lives miserable by giving them two choices they both hated. It was impossible for Danny, who was thirteen years-old, to stand up against Roy. Jackie had just turned eleven and already planning on how he was going to kill Roy. Jackie uncovered his head and peered over the edge of the bed. "How are we going to do that?"

"Leave that up to me," said Roy. "Get dressed meet me outside—and don't forget the beer cans."

The boys got dressed, walked into the kitchen, got a couple plastic trash bags, and collected the crushed National Bohemian beer cans strewn all over the floor. They went outside and dumped the trash bags in a large plastic container, not seeing their stepfather until he yelled from the base of the building.

"Hey, you two! Over here!"

They looked in the direction of the cellar. Roy was swinging a huge sledgehammer into the brick foundation, smashing age-old bricks into pieces, dust and debris clouding the air. He blasted a four-foot hole, tossing the remaining bricks into a growing pyramid next to the opening.

"Okay, guys. Come over here."

Roy never served in the military, but he always imagined himself as a brave Marine overtaking a German stronghold. He saw the rats as pesky little German rodents be taken out of their machine gun bulkhead.

"Okay, you knuckleheads. Grab a couple bricks. Now, I'm going in with this hammer and chase these mothers out of their happy little home. When they come out—smash 'em with your bricks—and don't miss! These are big suckers and I don't want them getting away."

The boys stared at one another, dumbfounded. Having no choice, Danny and Jackie grabbed two bricks apiece, reluctantly shuffling over to the pile.

"Wait a minute," said Roy. "Danny, come over here and look at this."

Danny dropped his bricks, cautiously creeping to the entrance. Roy leaned halfway into the cellar, the hammer still in his hand.

"Look at those creatures, will ya?"

Danny peered into the blackness of the hole. He couldn't see anything, but then a splinter of light shining through a floorboard revealed a nest of baby rats huddling together, squirming like tiny pink piglets. They actually looked cute to Danny. Suddenly, Roy swung his hammer, crushing the litter of rat pups, bursting a shower of baby rat flesh in their faces. Danny staggered backwards nearly fifteen feet, slammed into the neighbor's fence, and slid down the side, his legs buckling underneath him as he hit the ground. He rolled over, wiping his face with his sleeve. Then he threw up.

Jackie rushed over to him. "Are you all right?"

Danny stared up at Jackie, woozy and disoriented, glassy white eyes rolling around as if he was punch drunk.

Roy hollered across the yard, "Come on, you little punks! Get your bricks! I'm going in! Get ready for these bastards!"

Jackie helped his brother off the ground. Danny wiped his mouth again while Jackie slapped bits of pulverized baby rats off his shirt. Jackie glared at Roy, thinking about a phrase he had heard from his mother: "If looks could kill." For a few seconds, Jackie tried to kill Roy by glaring at him. It did not take long to realize Roy was not going to die from his death stare.

"I said come on, punks!" screamed Roy.

The two youngsters shambled back to the entrance, obediently picked up their bricks, and waited sheepishly outside the gaping hole.

Roy squeezed his body through the opening, started wailing away with the hammer. In a flash, a dozen angry rats stormed out of the hole, scurrying over the ground as if the basement was on fire.

"You're missing them! You're missing them!" yelled Roy. "You little pissants! Hit the fuckers!"

Jackie tried to hit one of the rats. but missed badly. Then he grabbed another brick and missed again, backtracking the whole time, hoping he wouldn't hit any of them. He glanced over at Danny who had morphed into a frozen lawn statue, his arms outstretched, gripping the bricks as if they were seared into his hands.

"Goddamn it! You punks are worthless! You didn't hit one of them! Danny, you little shithead! What are you? A fuckin' mummy? Christ almighty, get back in the house! Pieces of shit... pieces of shit..."

Betty woke the kids up. She shushed them with her index finger to keep them quiet. She had packed the barest necessities. The bags were placed next to the front door. She could hear the soft shuffling of bare feet on the floors as the kids were getting ready. Monica, Danny, and Jackie moved like clever little kittens around the house, getting dressed and gathering their things. They met Betty at the door. Then Betty and the kids sneaked out of the house, breathing in the brisk early morning air, waiting for Uncle Willie to arrive and make their escape.

Roy woke up early with a terrible hangover. At first, he did not notice anything unusual. Betty was not in bed, so he figured she must be making coffee. He went to the bathroom and then walked towards the kitchen. Betty was not there either. Maybe she's in Monica's room, he thought. Roy had been in her room before in the middle of the night. He peeked into Monica's room and saw an empty bed. For the first time, Roy became concerned. He bolted back to the other bedroom, looking for the boys. Now it was clear: the bastards had deserted him.

The first thing he destroyed was the couch in the living room. He took a butcher knife and ripped the couch to shreds, pausing only to throw one of his shoes through the TV. He began crushing all the furniture, slamming his foot through several pictures, breaking every mirror in the house. He shoved the refrigerator over on its side, spilling all the contents on the floor. Finally, Roy slumped on the floor exhausted, but already plotting what he was going to do to them after he found them.

Roy did not know it, but the family was moving swiftly away from him. They were riding comfortably in Uncle Willie's new Chevrolet Bel Air along Highway 95 North, thankful to be free at last and anxious to begin a new life in New Jersey.

As she gazed out the passenger window at the open fields, meadows, and farmlands along the highway, Betty felt a welcome surge of relief and optimism. Things were finally going to get better. Life without Roy would be safer, more enjoyable, and her children's future would be happy and secure. It would turn out to be a fleeting moment of hope. Unknown to Betty, Monica was four weeks pregnant.

In the back seat, Monica was looking the huge expanse of the Delaware Memorial Bridge, and the black plumes of smoke billowing from the smokestacks of the nearby DuPont factories. She felt a rare moment of peace and tranquility, but this too would be fleeting. Monica did not know she was pregnant either.

Danny was sleeping contentedly. Jackie was quiet in the backseat, thinking about how pleased he was to get away from his stepfather. He thought about Roy's violent fit of anger over a small portion of peas and how close he had been to that kitchen knife. Just a few more inches and he could have sliced that bastard's guts open. The thought of seeing Roy lying on the kitchen floor bleeding to death made him feel oddly serene. As Uncle Willie drove across the bridge into the flatlands of New Jersey, Jackie continued to enjoy thinking about the day he would return to Baltimore and plunge a knife into that worthless piece of shit.

*Twenty Years Later*

Jackie had no trouble finding Roy Shifflette. He still lived in the same brick row house that Betty had bought more than twenty years before.

23

Jackie had been watching Roy's movements—or lack of them—for two days, staking out the house from a rented room across the street. His 1965 silver Corvette was parked around the corner in a public parking lot. Jackie was taking no chances that Roy might become suspicious of a new classic sports car in the neighborhood.

Roy spent most his time sitting in his tattered, broken easy chair, which had only three legs and propped up on one side by a cinder block. The house still contained other demolished remnants of Roy's rampages. The refrigerator was badly dented and leaning awkwardly to one side. Shattered picture frames and shards of glass were strewn over the floor. Ripped seat cushions in one wing back chair still exposed coiled, rusted metal springs. An upside-down coffee table with three legs sticking up was leaning against the wall. In his raging fit, Roy forgot that he didn't have any money to replace the items he destroyed. He did manage to replace the busted TV and bought a used couch from the Salvation Army.

Roy's days were spent watching TV, eating junk food, and drinking cheap beer and whiskey until he passed out. Empty cans of National Bohemian beer, bottles of Wild Turkey, and leftover containers of potato chips, peanuts, Cheez Whiz, and Spam circled the chair, forming Roy's own personal trash dump. When he wasn't passed out, Roy glared at the TV, cursing the actors in the show, his former bosses at Bethlehem Steel, those fuckin' Yankees everywhere, and especially his wife Betty and her pieces-of-shit kids.

The two decades after Betty and the kids escaped had not been kind to Roy. The years were marked with an unending series of drunken acts of stupidity, hare-brained decisions, random acts of violence, child abuse, and miniature disasters that all added up to a big zero. Roy had long since been fired from his job at Bethlehem Steel for hitting one of his fellow workers in the back of the head with a board when he wasn't looking. Occasionally, he would ride around the city hoping to run into Betty, but he had no idea where she was or how to find her. He was still thinking about all the ways he was going to punish her and the kids for abandoning him in the middle of the night.

Roy stayed in the house despite hating his black neighbors. He fought with them constantly and called them names while everybody wondered why he didn't move to another neighborhood—a much whiter neighborhood. But, Roy took perverse pleasure in taunting the other residents and somehow maintained the illusion that he was superior to his black neighbors based on the fact that he was white and they were not. Roy enjoyed beating up defenseless women and children, and whenever he got the chance, he would grab a local youngster, slap him around, and then lie to the child's parents when questioned about the incident.

Roy had not had a full-time job in twenty years. He got by with part-time employment in machine shops, doing odd jobs, and a number of petty thefts, scams, and capers. Betty had paid for the house, so Roy was content to make enough money to keep the lights, heat, and water turned on and continue his supply of TV dinners, booze, and cigarettes.

At night he cruised along Eastern Avenue, checking out the prostitutes or stop to drink at one of the numerous sleazy shot-and-a-beer bars. When he had a little extra money, Roy loved to hang out at the Block, the notorious home of Baltimore's version of aristocratic French society. At one time the Block was a fairly respectable, high-class downtown burlesque district. In the old days, the area had exuded a certain kind of gilded-age charm and a noted stopover for famous exotic dancers and strippers like Blaze Starr.

Now, the Block was reduced to seedy sex shops and gaudy neon strip clubs with big-haired women in florescent bikinis exhorting passers-by to come in and gaze at a parade of big tits and heart-shaped asses snaking seductively around stripper poles. If that wasn't to your liking, you could also sample the transvestite musicals, dance performances, and peep shows where—for a price—you could ogle naked women unveiled behind drawn curtains.

Roy spent as much time as he could on the Block, but he rarely had enough money to stay very long. He found himself spending more and more of his nights cruising the gay bars and clubs in the city. Roy hated homosexuals almost as much as black people. But he thought he had discovered an ingenious way to keep himself in booze and cigarette money. He called it "rolling queers for fun and profit, as simple as dialing for dollars." He pretended he was gay and sucker guys at the bar into meeting him later in one of the darkened parking lots of the Inner Harbor. Roy made sure nobody at the bar ever saw him leave with another man, and they always took separate cars. Even though he did not consider himself gay, Roy would allow the man to give him a blowjob before Roy punched him out and ripped him off.

On the third night, Jackie saw Roy leave the house and followed him to one of the local bars. He sat discreetly in the back for more than an hour, watching Roy chatting up one of the men at the bar. Then Roy made a clumsy attempt to hide the fact that he was leaving the bar to meet the man, a skinny, nervous-looking guy with dark circles under his eyes. They left separately, minutes apart. Jackie stayed in the bar for a couple hours; neither man returned.

On the fourth night, Roy left for another bar. This time Jackie tailed him in his car after he left the bar to find out where they made the hookup.

Roy drove down to Pete's Bar in Fells Point, a hipster hangout noted for its ragtag barfly clientele. Pete's was home to an odd assortment of unemployed locals, struggling artists, lost poets, drug addicts, winos, male prostitutes, street-corner philosophers, and half the newspapermen at the *Baltimore Sun.* It was a narrow, funky bar containing a single row of bar stools upholstered in prison gray plastic with discolored cotton balls squeezing out the seams like puss from a pimple. A few stained card tables and rickety folding chairs lined the perimeter of the bar. Pete Garrett, the bartender, was a heavyset ex-Marine sporting a grizzly salt and pepper beard and a Black Sabbath T-shirt with the message "Fuck More/Bitch Less" inscribed on the back. His body was covered with dozens of vivid tattoos, but he said the lettering on his left bicep was his favorite: Eat Shit and Die. Pete maintained he liked most of his customers, except "that asshole Shifflette."

At the moment, the asshole was talking to a short, balding, fat, sweaty man with a round face and a pink complexion who looked like he just finished his first tanning session. Jackie thought he was a dead ringer for Porky, the Pig's father. They had a few drinks together, and after an hour, the pink fellow got up and left the bar, nodding to Roy shifty-eyed, as if he was a double agent on a secret mission.

Minutes later, Roy left the bar and walked to his faded brown 1972 Dodge Coronet. Jackie followed him, sat in his car, and waited until he headed out of Fell's Point towards the Inner Harbor. On South Broadway, he turned left on Pratt Street, pulled into the parking lot of the National

Aquarium, drove around to the back of the building, and parked next to another car.

Jackie parked his car on Pratt Street, grabbed the camera beside him, and walked stealthily along the cobbled pathway of Pier 4 directly across from the aquarium. He found a deserted spot behind a wooden billboard advertising Maryland crabs. A misty, shroud of dense fog rolled in from the harbor, making it difficult to discern the two cars, one of which was Roy's, and the other presumably Roy's victim for the evening. Jackie heard a car door open and close. Seconds later, another car door opened and closed. Jackie figured one of the men got in the other car. Ten minutes later, he spotted Pinky stumbling out of the shadows, clutching his side before collapsing in the parking lot. Grabbing his camera, Jackie took several shots of the man lying on the ground. Then Roy appeared out of the shadows, running awkwardly side-to-side as if he was blind drunk, seizing Pinky by the shoulders, and dragging him towards his car. Jackie repeatedly clicked the camera until the two men disappeared into the fog. Something had gone wrong. Jackie figured Roy was probably too drunk to make his assault and Pinky tried to escape.

Jackie ran back to his car and waited for Roy to leave. Soon, Roy wheeled his rust-bucket Dodge onto Pratt Street. Jackie continued following him as he made several turns before heading for the corner of North Fulton and West Fayette. He turned down Fulton, and drove a few blocks before stopping beside an empty weed-infested field adjacent to an empty warehouse.

Jackie could not imagine what Roy would be doing in the black part of town, parking his car in the middle of nowhere. Turning down a side street, he pulled into the driveway of an abandoned row house. He left his car, sneaked up behind a boarded-up storefront, peeking around the corner to see Roy bending down and removing the back license plate from his car; then he turned around and quickly removed the one in front. Roy began walking directly towards Jackie, the plates tucked under his arm. Ducking back from the building, Jackie sprinted to his car and jumped in seconds before Roy turned the corner, passing him on the other side of the street without noticing him. Jackie waited a few minutes, then sped away.

The next afternoon Jackie entered Millie's All-Nite Diner down the street. He picked up a copy of the *Baltimore Sun* and took a seat next to a burly, toothless construction worker clad in patchy denim overalls. A short, stumpy matron with a wad of stringy gray hair wrapped tightly in a bun plodded down the aisle as if trudging through a pool of molasses. She stood impatiently in front of Jackie clutching a yellow pad, reaching for a pencil sticking out of her hair.

"Whaddayahave?" slurred the waitress.

"Just coffee and a piece of apple pie."

"That's it?"

"Yeah, that's it."

The surly waitress slid the pencil in her hair, then turned and waddled back to the cook's station.

As he was waiting for his order, Jackie casually glanced at the front page of the paper, taking notice of a news story in the lower right-hand corner:

Man Stabbed to Death in Car at Inner Harbor

Baltimore police are investigating the discovery of the body of an unidentified man found slumped in the front seat of a 1972 Chevrolet in the parking lot of the National Aquarium in the Inner Harbor. Aquarium security officer William Dennings discovered the body early this morning when he arrived to work. Investigating officer Sergeant Percy Grimes said the man was stabbed numerous times, and no weapon was found on the scene. So far, the police have no suspects or motive for the killing. Sergeant Grimes is asking anyone with any information about the killing to contact the Baltimore Police Department.

Jackie jerked the paper close to his face, startling the construction worker. As he was re-reading the article, the bad-tempered waitress returned and placed his order on the counter. Quickly, Jackie withdrew three dollars from his pocket, tossed them on the counter, and rushed out of the diner as if he had spotted a spider crawling on top of his pie.

By the time he arrived back at his room, he already knew his next move. The first stop would be the A&P Supermarket two blocks down the street.

The next night Jackie found Roy sitting alone in Pete's bar. Roy had arrived after paying a pole dancer at the Two-Timers club fifty dollars for fifteen minutes worth of insincere conversation and a bottle of cheap watered-down champagne. The bouncers threw him out when he couldn't come up with another fifty dollars.

Roy was nursing a Pabst Blue Ribbon when Jackie sidled up to him. Roy turned and gave a quick glance to a man in his early thirties with sandy blond hair and a scruffy reddish beard.

"Mind if I sit down?" Jackie asked.

"Seat's open," said Roy.

Pete came over, and Jackie ordered a Budweiser.

Jackie said, "Hey, I'm Paul. I'm new in town. Just here for a few nights."

"Really…" muttered Roy. It was neither a question nor an invitation for further conversation.

"You from around here?"

"Yeah—but not originally."

"Oh? Where are you from?"

"Clarksburg, West Virginia."

"Hey, great town. I'm from Toledo, Ohio."

"Yeah, I heard of it."

"Look," said Jackie, "I only have a short time. I was wondering if you'd like to go for a ride with me."

Roy couldn't believe his luck. Normally, it took some time and a lot of bullshit to get these fags out of the bar. "Sure—after you pay for these beers. You're buying, right?"

Before he could answer, Pete came back and set a Bud in front of Jackie.

"Oh. yeah, no problem." said Jackie, tossing Pete a five-dollar bill.

"Listen," said Roy, "We can go after these beers, but we have to go in your car. You got a car, right?"

"Yes, it's in the parking lot."

"Well, I'm not meeting you there. I'll be waiting down the corner—in front of Murphy's bar."

"Sounds good to me."

The men polished off their beers and then left separately. Jackie drove down the block and picked up Roy.

"Nice car," said Roy.

"It's a beaut," Jackie said.

"My car's in the shop."

"No problem."

Jackie drove Roy to a darkened secluded area by the Inner Harbor, lighted only by glittering gold moonbeams reflecting off the water and the ships moored in the harbor. Jackie pulled off the road, easing the Vette into the back lot of a flour company.

He shut off the engine.

"Look," said Roy, impatiently, "Can we get this over with? How about sucking my cock?"

"Sure, Roy."

Roy was opening his fly when a stunned look of alarm spread across his face. "Wait a minute! How did you know my name?"

"You weren't that hard to find, Roy—you wife-beating son of a bitch."

"What the—"

The knife was an inch away from Roy's throat before he could finish.

"Look at me, motherfucker! You know, without the beard!"

"I don't know you—"

"Look at me! You know who I am!"

Roy stared into Jackie's murderous eyes. "Oh shit. Fuckin' Jackie."

"Put your hands behind your back."

Jackie tied Roy's arms with a piece of thick rope, then propped him up in the passenger seat. "So you remember that little kid you used to kick around like he was your own personal punching bag?"

"What are you going to do?"

Jackie reached back, slugged Roy senseless with his left fist, then got out of the car and came around to the other side. He opened the door, grabbed Roy by the shirt, and hurled a savage left hook to his face. Roy's nose gushing rivulets of blood by the time he fell out of the car, landing with a thud on the asphalt. Jackie bound his feet together and gagged him with duct tape. Roy was defenseless, curled in a fetal position, jerking his hands and feet, desperately trying to free himself.

Jackie opened the car door, seized two heavy plastic bags from the backseat, and dragged them over to Roy. Roy's eyes ballooned the size of fifty-cent pieces. Jackie towered over Roy, feeling the metallic burn of outrage lodged in the back of his throat. Jackie wanted to cut this bastard's heart out and throw it in the harbor. Instead, he went to the back of the car, reached into the trunk, and picked up a crowbar. He calmly strolled back to Roy who was writhing on the ground, rolling in the dirt, and squirming on his back like a wet dog.

"First of all, Roy, I want to tell you how lucky you are. I want you to know that I really want to plunge this knife into that empty shell of a heart you have. But I am not going to do it. You see, Roy, a real man knows about anger—knows when to show it and how much to show it. And—more importantly for you—who to show it to. You're not a real man, so I don't expect you to understand. You're a pathetic, ignorant, coward who beats up women and children. So I'm going to let you live because sticking a knife into you is not the proper way to channel my feelings of anger. Hey Roy, I'm sure you'll agree that we need to live in a civilized society. I'll let other people in authority give you the proper punishment. But really now, I don't think the cops are going to think kindly of you stabbing that poor man to death down here the other night. So let me see…what should be the proper way to express my anger?"

With the crowbar clutched in his hand, Jackie reared back and brutally crushed one of Roy's kneecaps, the nasty sound of cracking bones echoing clear out to the boats in the harbor. Roy doubled up in agony, rolled over on his stomach, his eyes bulging grotesquely out of his head.

"Say Roy, that felt pretty good. I think it's okay to express my anger even more, don't you?"

Once more Jackie raised the crowbar above his head, then slammed it down on Roy's other kneecap, sending him spiraling into painful convulsions.

"That should about do it, Roy. I'm finished with you for good."

Then Jackie bent down, picked up the two plastic bags, opened them, and turned them upside down, dumping the green slushy contents on top of Roy.

"Goodnight, Roy. Make sure you finish eating all your peas."

## Murder Suspect Found Covered in Peas

In a bizarre twist in the murder investigation of Charles McCamey, Baltimore resident Roy Shifflette was found this morning bound and gagged in the back lot of Pennington's Flour Company in the Inner Harbor district covered with gallons of canned peas.

Charles McCamey of Arbutus, Maryland, was stabbed to death last Thursday night in his car behind the National Aquarium. Operating on an anonymous tip, Baltimore police Sergeant Percy Grimes said they were told that Shifflette murdered McCamey and where he could be found. Shifflette was found lying in the parking lot with his hands and feet bound and tape covering his mouth. He also had two broken kneecaps.

Police said they had received more information that McCamey was stabbed to death in McCamey's car and that Shifflette abandoned his bloody car near the corner of N. Fulton and W. Fayette Streets. Sergeant Grimes said the department followed the lead and found a 1972 Dodge Coronet believed to belong to Shifflette. The front seat of the car contained numerous blood stains. Police also found several photos of Shifflette assaulting McCamey in the parking lot. In addition, Police found a concealed knife in Shifflette's pants, which is believed to be the murder weapon.

Sergeant Grimes was asked if he had any idea who the informant was or why Shifflette was drenched in buckets of peas.

"I have no idea," said Grimes. "You work here long enough and you think you've seen everything, and then something like this comes along. We believe we got our man, and that's the main thing."

# There's a Moon Out Tonight

Bien Hoa Province,
South Vietnam
August, 1967

Corporal Louie Foreman's nerves were rattled, torn, and frayed and his body exhausted after marching all day in the relentless torrential rain, leading his tired squad slogging over the water-soaked ground and sucking muck of the deep, gloomy jungle. It seemed like days since he had seen the full blazing sun. At this hour, he only glimpsed occasional slivers of sunlight streaking down through the tops of wide-leafed trees and spiraling vegetation. With Louie on point, the twelve men behind him marched with their heads down, trudging slowly through the deep brush, snarling vines, and thick trees, grunting and groaning, swinging their machetes and KA-BARs. As the darkening sky signaled the coming of night, Louie thought the jungle was actually getting thicker and denser as his men stomped, slid, sweated, cursed, and hacked their way through the unending masses of tangled thickets and banyan trees. The men's hands were raw and blistered, their bodies fighting insects, leeches, fatigue, and muscle pain, trying to forge a narrow path through the heavy jungle.

The temperature rose steadily reaching a hundred degrees during the day, followed by unexpected bursts of rainfall that dropped temperatures lower than thirty degrees at night. The men marched methodically without speaking, looking more like prisoners on a chain-gang than men at war. Louie had never understood the phrase "blanket of humidity" until he went to Vietnam. The blanket weighed down every ounce of their equipment, dehydrated them, and made the marching slow and tortuous, like trying to walk through a valley of Jell-O. Some of the men took off their jackets and shirts completely to avoid overheating and make it easier to locate leeches.

Louie regularly rotated each fire team because after a couple hours their psyches were frazzled by the constant nervous tension of being on point. The bleeding blisters on his feet stung every time he lifted his boots out of the sucking mud. He estimated that they had traveled a mere hundred meters in the last two hours, and if they didn't find some kind of natural shelter soon, they would have to spend another night huddled under their nylon ponchos in the drenching rain.

Louie glanced behind him and saw Franconia from fire team two flailing away at a swarm of mosquitoes swirling around his helmet. "Jesus Christ!" Franconia screamed. "These fuckin' mosquitoes are the size of Buicks!" The young Marine stopped in his tracks, flung his KA-BAR on the ground, and reached into his rucksack. "Corporal!" cried Franconia, hollering up the column to Louie. "I need to get some more bug juice!"

Louie turned around, facing exhausted, shadowy figures on the brink of collapsing. "No problem, Franconia. "I think we could all use a break. Let's set up in this area for the night. Maybe the rain will let up tomorrow."

The rain continued its steady downpour as the men cleared a small area and strung their green ponchos together with wire between two large trees. They happily dropped their rucksacks, canvas tarps, shovels, M-16s, machetes, and KA-BARs to the ground and then removed their helmets, shirts, and boots. PFC Anderson flung his heavy M-60 machine gun into the mud, grunting as if he was lifting a refrigerator off his back. Everyone grabbed their canteens, gulping water voraciously while reaching for insect repellent, anxious to rid their bodies of sickening leeches that literally fell on them from the trees. A few of the men reached for combat rations or lit cigarettes, unconcerned that the tips might be seen by Vietcong in the area. Bravo One had told them there was no enemy in the vicinity, and an ambush was very unlikely at this point in the mission. To the men this was hardly consoling, since most of the enlisted Marines viewed the top brass as rich college kids who came over as second lieutenants right out of basic school in Quantico. The officers and lifers were the guys who opted out to be commanders of weapons platoons, holed up safely at a company command post, eating three squares a day, deciphering maps, locating enemy ammunition dumps, or planning imaginary strategies for victory.

This was one reason the enlisted men respected Corporal Foreman. He was a fighter who wanted to kill the enemy, not spend the day sticking pushpins in a map or sitting at a typewriter ordering Marines to their deaths.

But it didn't matter. If they were ambushed now, they'd be dead anyway. They didn't have enough fire power, the strength to fight, and there was no immediate backup.

Louie squatted in the mud, pulled a Lucky Strike out of his shirt pocket, lit it, and held it between his teeth as he removed his boots. The blisters were red, purple, and pulsating, the size of fifty-cent pieces. He rolled up his fatigues and was not surprised to discover three bloody red leeches attached to his legs. He pulled the leeches off his legs and burned them with his cigarette lighter. He made a mental note to ask one of the men to check his back for any others. He wondered why he could not feel them sucking his blood like vampire worms and why God would permit such a creature to exist on earth, since he could not think of a reason for their existence. He was rubbing his toes, thinking about oiling his M-16, when Private Gonzalez from fire team three approached him, soaking wet, his helmet tilted back on his head.

"Corporal, sir?"

"Yes, Gonzalez. What is it?"

"It's Private Dempsey. I think you should have a look."

Louie put his boots back on, strained to get up, and grabbed his helmet out of habit. He followed Gonzalez, sloshing through the line of ponchos in his rolled up fatigues.

Louie and Gonzalez arrived at fire team three's lean-to and saw two men hunched over another Marine.

"What's the problem?" asked Louie.

One of the men whispered, "It's Dempsey, Corporal. Look at his feet."

Louie took out his flashlight and shined it down on the young Marine, who was propped against a tree with his pants up to his knees, his socks off and his feet exposed.

Louie peered through the red beam of light and then fought the urge to throw up. He swallowed hard, trying not to look overly concerned about Dempsey's feet which were dark blue, swollen twice their size, and covered with open sores and ugly ulcers. His toes looked like they were rotting off.

"Jesus Christ," said Louie. "He's got jungle rot."

"Jungle rot?" asked one of the men.

"Immersion foot—old-timers call it trench foot," explained Louie. "It's from the marching... in the sweat, cold, and damp."

Dempsey gazed up at Louie, squinting in the quickening darkness. "I'm sorry, sir. They're pretty bad, huh?"

"Dempsey, what the hell were you thinking?" demanded Louie, bending down to examine Dempsey's feet. Louie saw white pus oozing from the ulcers and fungal infections already spreading upward beyond his ankles. "How on earth have you made it this far? Why didn't you say something?"

"I don't know," replied Dempsey. "I didn't want to complain... I didn't want to slow us down."

Louie turned to Gonzalez. "Get me Jackson right away. Tell him to meet me at team one's position—pronto."

Louie stood up and switched off his flashlight. "Dempsey, you hang loose, you hear? Rogers, get some clean bandages or anything else that might help from the medical kits."

"Aye, aye, Corporal," said Rogers, running down the line, imploring the men to dig into their rucksacks for any clean bandages or disinfectant of any kind.

Louie returned to his hooch, followed closely by Jackson, who ran up to him with his bulky PRC-25 strapped to his back, scratchy sounds emanating from the handset. Louie sat down in the mud and leaned back against a tree, the rain poring over the lip of the poncho just beyond his feet. He switched on his flashlight and pulled a map out of his flak jacket pocket. "Get me the CO of Bravo One actual. His code name is Rolls Royce." ordered Louie.

Jackson flipped a switch on the handset. "Bravo One, this is Red Dog DiMaggio. Come in. Repeat. Come in, Bravo One. Red Dog DiMaggio."

"Come in, Red Dog. We hear you."

"Bravo One. Character Chevy Two actual needs to speak with Character Rolls Royce actual. Over."

"Roger that, Red Dog. Is this an emergency?"

"Roger that, Bravo Two. Over."

"Hold on, Red Dog. Out."

Louie waited a few minutes before he recognized the voice of second-lieutenant James Edwardson, the platoon commander.

"This is Character Rolls Royce actual. What's the trouble?"

Louie grabbed the handset. "Character Rolls Royce, this is Character Chevy Two. We have a bad situation here. One man down with jungle rot on both feet, gangrene setting in quickly. Over."

"Is he going to make it? Over."

"No, sir. We need a medivac chopper and a corpsman on the double. Over."

"Shit, Chevy Two. Our fuckin' birds are all up and down the D Zone right now in the middle of a major shit storm. They're bringing in dozens of wounded and casualties—a lot worse than feet amputation. Over."

Louie gritted his teeth, trying to sound rational. "Sir, we need more than medical help. We've been humping our asses off all day, and we need food, water, medical supplies, power sources for radios, bug juice—we're running out of everything. Over."

"Roger that, Chevy Two. What are your coordinates?"

"From Pepsi, up two-point-four and right three-point-one. Over."

"Wait one second, Chevy Two. Over."

Louie waited a few minutes before the platoon commander's scratchy voice returned "Chevy Two actual, come in."

"Chevy Two actual here."

"We got a CH-46 due to unload at 1900 hours, if he makes it here. He'll need an LZ. You're in the thick of it. Over."

"Roger that, Rolls Royce. Let me check the map for a clear zone. Will get back with you. Over."

Louie handed the handset to Jackson and unfolded his map. The paper map was a confusing series of contour lines indicating longitude, latitude, uneven terrain, and small villages, but some of the lines did not even join together. Even the damn mapmakers didn't know the whole country. Louie knew the squad was currently located in a valley heading for the high country, but the really steep mountains were still farther north. The chopper would be taking a chance by coming in over high ground, but if the sky was clear, Louie felt they could get one of the birds over the crest of one of the smaller mountains. The problem was building a landing zone for the helicopter. The jungle was too thick, and his men were too tired to clear trees and bushes. They needed to find a meadow or farmland with elephant grass as their worst enemy. Louie noticed the map showed a level contour in between two lines that did not join about 450 meters due east. With any luck, the blank spaces would mean a rice paddy or meadow. Louie figured this was Dempsey's only chance to save his feet. If they could reach the landing zone area and clear it by morning, he would have a decent chance of going back home, starting a new life, and taking dancing lessons.

"Jackson, get me Character Rolls Royce actual back on."

Within a few seconds, the CO responded. "Character Rolls Royce here."

"Character Rolls Royce, this is Chevy Two. We found a good place for an LZ at Coca-Cola up five-point-seven, left nine-point-one. Over."

"That's near Binh Gia. We bombed the shit out of that area. That whole place is loaded with water-filled bomb craters from B-52 strikes. Nothing but farmland and the remains of a village—should be abandoned by locals, but you never know."

"Roger on that. We'll be on the lookout. Over."

"We can't get there before 2200 hours. Over."

"No problem. We'll be waiting. Over."

"Chevy One, we can't delay your mission any longer than this. Charlie Company is putting the fuckin' squeeze on me. Over."

"Roger that, Rolls Royce. We're committed to the mission. We still have time. Over."

"Let's hope so. Good luck, Chevy Two. Over and out."

Louie handed the handset to Jackson and put the map back in his jacket pocket. He realized his squad would have to do some serious humping through the jungle to get to the drop area by morning. His men were already exhausted, and he wasn't sure how they would react to diverting a mission and marching all night for the sake of one Marine. He called out to Jackson, "Tell the men to meet in fire team one's hooch in fifteen minutes. No delays."

"Yes, Corporal," replied Jackson.

Fifteen minutes later, Corporal Foreman was standing before his drenched squad huddling tightly together like a cluster of tired seals. With the coming of night the temperature had dropped, and some of the men were shivering, their arms folded tightly together. A few smoked cigarettes.

Two guys were sharing a can of combat rations. None of them looked like they were in the mood to march all night.

"Listen, men. All of you have seen Dempsey's condition. It's a bad case of immersion foot—the worst I've ever seen. If we don't get him out of here in eight hours, the gangrene will do him in. I contacted Bravo One, and they can get us a chopper here around 2200 hours."

"Did you say *here?*" asked Atkins, one of the members of fire team two.

"No," said Louie. "There's no way to clear an LZ near here. I checked the map. There's a clearing about five hundred meters due east."

"So," said Private Sanders, tossing a cigarette into the ground, "We need to hump all night."

"That's right," said Louie.

There was a brief moment of silence.

"Well," said Sanders, "What the fuck are we waiting for?"

"Nothing, Sanders. Everybody get their gear. We move out in ten minutes."

The squad resumed hacking and cutting their way through the thick brush. It was normally pitch black, but the trees had thinned out, and a full yellow moon was casting enough light for the men to see a couple feet in front of them.

Louie turned his head around and spoke to Private Williams, who was marching right behind him.

"Hey, Private Williams! You ever hear of a song called, 'There's a Moon Out Tonight' by the Capris? It came out around 1958."

"Yes," said Williams. "It was a make-out song, wasn't it?"

"You bet it was."

Louie turned back around and continued plodding through the thicket. After a few minutes, Williams called out to his squad leader, "Why did you ask me that, Corporal?"

"You ever go to the sock hops when you were a kid?" Louie asked.

"Yeah," said Williams. "They were great."

"We had ours at a community center, and they had this really cool deejay. He played the best records—"

"And you remember dancing with a cutie to 'There's a Moon Out Tonight'?"

"Yeah, it's that damn moon… reminds me of stuff I need to forget about right now. Takes you to the wrong place…"

Louie resumed his steady chopping with his machete. Williams was about to mention his own cutie from junior high but remained silent, sensing that reminding Corporal Foreman of beautiful memories right now might not be such a good idea.

As the late-night march wore on, the jungle remained spooky and silent except for a chorus of exotic birds making high-pitched, eerie sounds like a dissonant symphony from sirens in Greek mythology. After fifty meters, Dempsey was unable to walk even with one of his fellow Marines holding him up. Finally, the men took turns carrying Dempsey piggyback while another Marine cleared the path in front of them.

As he was tramping through the bush in a kind of self-induced hypnosis, Louie was thinking about all the different ways you could die in Vietnam. Sure, the gooks could wipe you out with rifles, machine guns, grenades, bombs, and mortars, but that was only part of the equation. He was terrified he might piss off a venomous snake every time he took a step. He heard about a Marine who died after being sprayed in the eyes with venom from a king cobra. Louie knew about king cobras, but sprayed in the eyes six feet away? It was a good thing the Marines didn't have to tell the next-of-kin exactly how a Marine died. There were numerous other horror stories of men being eaten alive by tigers or crocodiles or succumbing to poisonous bites from an endless variety of reptiles, scorpions, lizards, and even some types of tree frogs. You could also step on one of the hundreds of land mines or un-exploded bombs waiting for your false step in the valleys and farmlands. Men also died from malaria, pneumonia, friendly fire, fragging, eating bad fish, or drowning in bombed-out craters. The ways to die seemed as infinite as the jungle itself. Louie knew a complete waste of humanity when he saw it, and for the life of him, he couldn't understand how the hell these random, stupid deaths had anything to do with containing Communism. But after all, like the poem said, his was not to reason why; his was but to do or die. Trying to reason things out only made you crazier.

After about 350 meters, the jungle thickets became less dense, the brush thinned out, and the trees became smaller. Louie could sense that they were nearing the perimeter of the jungle. Around daybreak, the beaten squad finally reached a clearing of tall grass and masses of matted bamboo stretching over fifty meters. It was tall grass, but it wasn't elephant grass, and Louie was relieved that the men could hack away without getting stinging cuts on their bodies. In the distance, Louie could see what the second lieutenant had told him about. There were several acres of farmland destroyed by giant round craters filled with dirty rain water. In the middle of the craters, he spotted a row of burned-out straw huts and the charred remnants of a stone building. A broken cross tilted to its side on top of the building. *Jesus,* he thought, *what the hell is a Christian church doing out here in the middle of nowhere?*

The men worked their sore bodies as hard as they could to clear an area for the helicopter to land. They slowly opened a patch of crumpled, twisted vegetation in the valley floor surrounded by dark green mountains towering above them on all sides. After two hours, Louie told them to put down their machetes and KA-BARs lie down, close their eyes, and pretend they were on R&R, getting laid in Hawaii. It wasn't much, but this space would have to do.

An hour later the squad heard the whirring blades of the chopper in the distance looming over the crest of one of the smaller mountains. A roaring sound reverberated through the valley like a cruise missile. The canyon was not very large, but it still blocked some of the transmissions from the PCR-25. Jackson was talking feverishly on the radio, giving the coordinates, tinny voices barking out of the handset. Louie overheard something scratchy that sounded like, "Your best approach is from the south. Zone's secure. Over."

The chopper came in fast, turned, and made its approach, setting down gently. The blades of the chopper lashed the puddles of water beneath it, splashing dirty water over the men. The rear jaws of the chopper opened. Two Marines ran out quickly with a stretcher and placed Dempsey on it, giving the squad an enthusiastic thumbs-up. Two other Marines tossed supplies out the open door, laughing and trying to make jokes above the din of the swirling blades. Louie's men grabbed the packages, and the tailgate immediately closed. They waved to pilot and crew as the chopper lifted quickly into the air, disappearing within seconds.

41

Louie tried to gather his men together, but they were laughing, joking, opening packages, and joyfully passing around cans of warm beer. Louie decided to wait a while until the men felt ready to return to their mission trail. Private Sanders wandered over towards the wasted village, carefully walking around several craters, peeking in to see if there were any bodies floating in the water. As he neared the village, he stood in front of the church, turned halfway around, and shouted back to his squad, "Hey, guys, I'm going to church!" Sanders looked up at the cross, dropped his rifle, placed his hands in prayer position, and kneeled down. "Please, Father, send me down a Thailand babe with big tits and a pile of money!"

Private Rogers screamed, "God doesn't listen to stupid Marines—he keeps those babes for himself!"

Sanders turned to walk into the church. But, he never got there. A bullet from a VC's AK-47 blew a hole in his heart. Sanders looked down at his chest, but before his eyes found the hole, he was dead, collapsing to the ground with a dreadful thud.

The Marines quickly grabbed their rifles and scrambled for cover. Louie immediately hollered for everyone to charge towards a nearby three-foot dike built up behind a rice paddy. Several other shots rang out, bullets whizzing by their heads. The frenetic squad all seemed to dive into the muddy dike at the same time, splashing water high into the air. Louie fell hard on his chest at the end of the line, raising his rifle on his shoulder. He was lying next to Private Elms.

"How many do you think there are?" asked Elms.

"I don't know. I could only make out scattered shots of AK-47s coming from three directions—but I know one thing."

"What's that?"

"We can't stay here and let them pick us off one by one. There's no cover for a retreat. We've got to clean them out!"

"Okay, listen up, men!" yelled Louie down the line at the leaders of each fire team. "Fire team two, you take the left flank! Circle around! Use the craters for cover, but find those motherfuckers! Fire team three! Take the right flank! Keep pushing ahead! I don't think there's too many of them. Don't be heroes! Just one crater at a time. Got it? Team one will head straight in."

Louie gathered his team around him.

"Okay, we're gonna be patient. Just one crater to the next—as fast as we can. Got it?"

The men nodded.

"Okay, follow me!"

Louie lunged out of the dike, heading for a crater about ten meters away. His three fellow Marines followed close behind. The other units moved forward, drawing fire, bullets cracking overhead as the M-16s, on full automatic, answered back with bursts of gunfire before the men leaped into an open wet crater. Louie continued firing rounds into the huts; they were still too far away for grenades. One VC was gunned down by Private Atkins as he tried to move from one bunker to another. Fire team three, dodging bullets all the way, managed to slip behind the enemy in back of the village, quickly opening fire. The VC were now in a crossfire, a firestorm of bullets hissing through the air. In the middle of the chaos, Private Elms, who was still lying beside Louie, yelled over at him, "Look at that!"

Peering over at the front of the church, he saw a young peasant woman scrambling for cover, a baby wrapped in her arms. Totally confused, she ran in one direction, then darted in another, searching desperately for a safe place to hide, caught between two enemies in mortal combat.

"Christ," mumbled Louie.

"Look at that fuckin' idiot!" screamed Elms. "Is that funny, or what?"

Louie looked again and understood what Elms was saying. She did look rather comical, like something you might see in one of those silent films with quick, jerky movements by the actors.

"Yeah, It's fuckin' hilarious."

"No shit," said Elms.

Elms aimed his rifle at the woman, shot her in the head, and then fired again, splitting the baby in half.

"Well, she's okay now! She's found a home! Right in front of a church!"

The woman and child lay lifeless and bloodied in the street.

Louie smiled broadly. "She sure has. That kid won't be killing any Americans—that's for sure!"

The fire teams quickly closed in and surrounded the snipers. They shot two enemies in one bunker, three more in another. Two others were gunned down trying to escape into the jungle.

Suddenly everything went quiet.

The men hunched down on their knees, rifles in hand, eyes darting swiftly from one spot in the jungle to another. They listened and watched carefully for any sound or movement, any hint of possible danger in front of them. After a few anxious moments, Louie signaled for his men to regroup and check out the wounded.

They were lucky. Private Armstrong suffered a bullet wound to his arm, and PFC Erickson had a bullet go right through his side. Both would be able to make it back to the mission site. Louie instructed Jackson to radio Bravo One to pick up Sanders. In the aftermath, the Marines were sitting quietly on the broken steps of the church. Before them lay blanket-covered Sanders covered with a blanket and the gruesome exposed dead woman and child.

"How the fuck did that happen?" asked Private Anderson as his arm was being wrapped.

"She obviously got hit by friendly fire, you idiot," said Elms, laughing out loud while swinging a burlap sack of eyeballs back and forth. "Besides, can't you see that AK-47 lying beside her? She was armed and dangerous!" Elms held up the sack for everyone to see. "I got six more today, brothers!"

"Right," said Anderson.

But he wasn't laughing. None of the men were laughing except Elms.

Louie stared at Elms and then looked at the woman and child. "Hey, Elms," commanded Louie. "Shut the fuck up. I'm gonna write your ass up—it's not funny."

"But you—"

"I *said* shut the fuck up, Private!"

"Yes, Corporal!"

Louie turned away from the church, gazing down at the scorched bottomland stretching as far as the eye could see, a blackened devastated wasteland devoid of any signs of life. No trees. No flowers. No birds. In the silence, a pale blue smokey mist settled over the land, drifting like a fog towards the imposing dark green mountains that lay beyond it all, far into the distance. He never felt more alone in his life. And for a few minutes, he was lost; he had no idea where he was, or who he was. He had slipped into an inexorable void, a black hole of existence, rendered bluntly desensitized, a mind completely devoid of cognition. He did not know how long his weary, rooted eyes stared forlornly at the barren countryside, but at some point a disembodied voice whispered in his ear.

"Corporal, are you all right?"

Louie glanced up at a young Marine who looked about fourteen-years-old.

"Of course, Private. Let's pull out."

# The Flat Man

Harry Miller stood in front of the Mazadan Country Club in Casablanca, Morocco admiring the impressive building modeled after an ancient Moorish castle. The architects had preserved age-old traditions like U-shaped arches, towering ramparts, and sturdy guard walls built to ward off pirates and foreign invaders. The majestic clubhouse was situated about fifty yards from the ocean, surrounded by lush green fairways, and lavish gardens festooned with rich and colorful flora.

It was a perfect day for golf; not a cloud in the sky. Harry carried his bag to the side of the building near a row of golf carts, braced it against a wooden fence. As he entered the clubhouse, he was instantly overwhelmed by the vaunted ceilings, painted and glazed ceramics, translucent silk curtains, and elegant furnishings reflecting pastel colors of turquoise, salmon, and androsy pink. Shining green and white tiling lined the walls and archways. Harry thought it looked more like the Palace of Versailles than a place to hit a little white ball into a hole.

Wandering around in a daze, he ran into the most munificent pro shop he had ever seen, articles of clothing, golf clubs, and golfing accessories spanning the large room for miles, forming a sparkling sea of bright colors, silver and glass. Behind a ceramic half-moon counter, he spotted a tall handsome man with perfectly coiffed dark hair, sharply dressed in black pants, white shirt and black bow tie. He looked more like a headwaiter at the Rainbow Room in New York than a pro shop manager.

"Can I help you?" He asked.

"Is Louis, the Fourteenth around?"

"I beg your pardon?"

"Just kidding. I'm Harry Miller. I have a twelve-fifteen tee time."

Following check-in, Harry arrived at the first tee. Nobody was in front or behind him. An elderly gentleman in yellow shorts and a blue shirt hopped out of a cart with a red flag on it, and took his receipt.

"Have you ever played the course before?" he asked.

"No."

"The course is easily maneuverable. Just follow the signs."

"Is there a ninety degree rule with the carts?"

"No, but stay away from the greens."

"Of course. Thanks."

"Have fun!" he exclaimed.

The course was easily maneuverable, but it was also tough. Aside from long holes, the fairways were narrow, swirling winds blew in from the ocean, and it was booby trapped with nasty water hazards and imposing sand traps. In the past, Harry would get extremely upset when he played lousy golf. When he first started playing, he expected to be a decent player. In his youth he had been a superior athlete with good hand-eye coordination. He figured if he could hit a baseball at 85 miles-an-hour, he could hit a golf ball that was *just sitting there.* But, playing lousy golf turned him into a raving maniac, a crazed lunatic, exploding with violent fits of anger after every bad shot (which was just about *every* shot).

Harry's tantrums went like this: He hollered, and he screamed, and he broke clubs, and he cursed the clubs, and he cursed the golf course, and he cursed the fairways, and he cursed the greens. He cursed the crummy weather, and he cursed the golf gods, and he cursed the regular God, and he cursed Allah, and he cursed Krishna, and he cursed Buddha, and he cursed Buddha's mother, and he cursed his mother for not giving him lessons when he was a kid. He cursed himself for taking up golf in the first place, and he cursed the Scottish bastards who invented this fucked-up game in the first place.

That was before he changed his whole attitude. Finally, it dawned on him that he was not going to be another Tiger Woods, deciding to relax, chill out, and not let a walk in the park be spoiled. Now, he was satisfied to let nature's impressions consume him by soaking in the refreshing cool breezes, majestic flights of seabirds soaring over the wild open sea, the breathtaking landscape, and gentle waves frothing in the sparkling blue-green ocean. Now, he took time to watch squawking seagulls diving headlong into the water, marveled at the wild assortment of vivid desert flowers like hollyhock, jasmine, and white oleander blooming along the fairways.

He rounded a sharp dogleg-right on the 14th hole and came upon a gorgeous green nestled among a grove of eucalyptus trees at the edge of a wooded area. The green was bordered by two shiny-white sand traps on the left and a small pond at the bottom of a sloping embankment on the right side. A big white stork perched on a boulder jutting out of the pond and he spotted a turtle the size of a Frisbee staring at him before scuttling into the water.

He was about 50 yards from the hole. He took out his pitching wedge and lined up his shot. As he stood over the ball, he glanced around; there was still nobody in back of him. It was eerily silent, broken only by the comforting trill of small birds flitting about in the woods. He put the wedge back into his bag, picked up the ball, and walked towards the green. The cathedral-like spectral hush reminded him of Buddha's quest for enlightenment, and how he found peace of mind appreciating the simple joys of nature.

When he reached the hole he dropped the ball into the cup, sat down and assumed a lotus position. For five minutes he mediated on the green, repeating his mantra, taking in solemn deep breaths. Then he quickly jumped up, grabbed the ball and returned to his cart, self-consciously embarrassed, wondering whatever possessed him to meditate like a Tibetan monk on a golf course green outside the city of Casablanca.

He finished up the round with a par on the 18th hole. Buoyed by the beauty of the course and the perfect weather, he decided to have a late lunch in the club's restaurant. Entering, he noticed that it was empty except for a chubby, round-faced bartender watching TV, and four guys eating at a table next to the bar. He sidled up to the bar, and grabbed a stool.

"Can I help you?" asked bartender whose neck was about to bust his bow-tie loose.

"How about a ham and cheese sandwich and a beer."

"Toasted or on a roll?"

"On a roll—with mayonnaise."

The bartender nodded, and then slipped into the back before returning and pouring a draft for Harry who was pretending to watch a soccer game on TV. He was close enough to overhear bits of conversation from the men at the table. At least two of them seemed to be Americans.

One of the guys sporting a bright red short-sleeve shirt appeared to be in his sixties with thinning red hair, and a wispy ruddy beard. He was more animated than the others, talking louder, and when he finished a sentence his voice rose several octaves, culminating in a boisterous laugh evolving into a high-pitched squeal. Harry swore he heard that laugh before. He hopped off the stool, heading for the men's room. As he passed the four guys, he looked closer at the fellow with the red hair and funny laugh. His nose seemed unnaturally flattened, and through the beard you could see the faint outline of a scar running below his nose, creating a white crease in his lip.

On the way back from the men's room, he stopped and stood in front of the men feeling like a complete dork, watching them as they gave him dirty looks.

"I'm sorry," Harry muttered, gaping at the guy with the scar. "But, you look familiar."

"Really?" he asked.

"Are you American?"

"Hell, yeah!" he exclaimed. "Who the fuck are you?"

"Look...I'm sorry I bothered you," Harry turned turned to leave.

"Wait a minute!" the man cried. "What's your name?"

"Harry Miller."

"Are you *fucking* kidding me! I'm Doug Sterris!"

"Doug Sterris!" cried Harry. "I can't believe it! What the hell are you doing here?"

"I'm on a business trip. Hey, sit down and join us! Bartender! Bring my old friend Harry Miller a drink!"

Doug introduced Harry to the other three men. One of them was Mike, a handsome well-built guy in his forties clad tan shorts, a green polo shirt, and a New York Yankees baseball cap. He did not catch the names of the other two men who were garbed in dark blue, finely tailored three-piece suits with patterned ties. They looked to be of Arab descent, and in addition to nice suits, wore identical black wrap-around sunglasses

49

and serious expressions on their faces. The two men glared at Harry as if he was a wired rat for the F.B.I. It occurred to Harry that this was an unusual foursome.

"Jesus," said Doug, "What are you doing in Casablanca?"

"I'm just passing through for a couple days. I'm heading to Lisbon, and then the southern coast of Portugal."

"For vacation?"

"Yeah, mostly. I took early retirement. I'm looking for a place to settle down."

"And you're alone?"

"I've been divorced for a year—and what are you doing here?"

"I'm doing business with these guys," said Doug, pointing at the two Arabs. "Mike and I came down from Tangiers yesterday."

"Are you living in Tangiers?"

"Temporarily. I move around a lot."

"So, you're a big-time businessman?"

"Shit no!" exclaimed Doug. I do some import/export stuff. These guys on the other hand," gesticulating to the two Arabs, "are the real big-time businessmen."

Harry nodded to the look-a-like suits who remained impassibly bored, but seemingly alert enough to tear his heart out if they so desired.

"So, you're retired," continued Doug. "What from?" "From teaching. I was a professor at a small college in South Carolina."

"What did you teach?"

"Sociology, English Lit, and some courses on film and music."

"Music? Like what?"

"Like stuff from your closet—Hendrix, The Who, Stones."

"Your closet?" interjected Mike.

"My roommate was an asshole," said Doug. "So, I grabbed my records and moved into a big closet in our room."

"That sounds like you," said Mike.

Doug bellowed his lusty-hearted laugh. "Oh yeah! And the other guys in the house thought I was anti-social because I was smoking pot. Of course I was anti-social! Nobody else smoked pot! It didn't take long for guys like this joker to come up and socialize with me. I couldn't get rid of them!"

Harry grinned. "And you're a golfer now?"

"Well," said Doug. "I *try* to play. Mike is the golfer at the table. We just finished a round a couple hours ago. He shot a 76."

"Wow, he's out of my league."

"He's out of mine too!" exclaimed Doug. "Listen, where are you staying?"

"The Novotel Hotel—center city near the train station."

"I know where it is. Listen Harry, we're just about to split. Let's get together tomorrow. I can show you the city!"

"Sounds good to me. I was hoping to check out Rick's Cafe."

"It's a nice place, but a total tourist trap."

"I know, but I'm still interested."

"Then you know Casablanca is nothing like the movie."

"I know. I caught a glimpse of it outside my window this morning."

"It's a real shit hole, but it's got some cool attractions. I'll show you a couple tomorrow. How about we meet at your hotel at one o'clock? We'll catch some lunch—and catch up on old times. It's been...What? Forty years?"

"Something like that."

"You look great, by the way."

"Thanks. I'm glad you're alive and well."

"But still crazy after all these years!" cried Doug, laughing boisterously in his own unmistakable way.

Doug was alone when he picked up Harry at the hotel. He was casually dressed in a pair of tan slacks, short-sleeved white shirt, and brown and white canvas shoes. A straw hat perched jauntily on his head. He looked like a well-to-do English gentleman vacationing abroad.

"Are you hungry?" he asked.

"Not particularly."

"Good. I want to show you something, then we can check out Rick's Cafe. Sound okay?"

"Sounds good to me."

Doug and Harry left the front entrance of the hotel which spilled out into a loud, bustling street crammed with idling cars and trucks embroiled in a dusty smoking traffic jam. After stepping outside the hotel, the ninety-five degree heat struck them like a blowtorch. In spite of the ritzy neighborhood, the stench of rotting fish oscillated in the air, powerful and persistent, as if it rising up from the bowels of the earth. Doug eyed Harry, reading his thoughts.

"It's the dead fish," he said. "Fishing and canning fish are the two biggest industries."

"It seems like something died besides fish,"

They ambled down the busy street for a few blocks before passing under a huge stone archway leading into the walled city of Old Medina. The ancient cobblestone streets turning bumpier, more narrow and crooked. The buildings and apartment houses bordering the walkways were faded white, gray, and brown. Signs of structural disintegration were everywhere. Glancing around, Harry spotted dry-rotted wooden buildings and arches, balconies peeling paint, and rusty ironwork decorating doors and windows. Withered, bleached out arabesque swirls adorned most of the structures, along with old-fashioned unreadable signage. Despite the overall decay, Old Medina, still maintained a certain irrepressible charm.

As they trudged up a steep incline, electric chords from an amplified guitar reverberated down the street, creating an ancient glimmering, jewel-like sound. The eerie instrumental reverb provided a perfect soundtrack for the bustling melody of life swirling all around the neighborhood. Old back-bent men trudged along pulling carts laden with fruits and vegetables, excitable raucous kids scrambled after a soccer ball, and doddering gray-haired women sat fanning themselves in the shade of fig trees. A bony, weedy-thin goat grazing on a piece of old newspaper solemnly glanced at Harry as if to ask, "What else are you going to do with an old newspaper?"

Old Medina was a vast array of souks lining the streets with an explosion of colors bursting from fabrics, rugs, dresses, hats, mosaic designs, weaving, ceramics, silver-plated teapots, leather handbags, and just about every other type of Moroccan handicraft. A few of the souks were heaped with spices releasing an orgy of pungency such as paprika, cinnamon, and saffron. Six wire cages hung on the wall housing live chameleons, cobras, salamanders, and one forlorn-looking bald eagle. Harry wanted to rip open the cages and set them free.

A slew of disparate people using variant modes of transportation flooded the street producing vertiginous commercial chaos. Street hawkers on foot, men on scooters, boys on bicycles, ancient bearded men dragging donkey carts, old, women hunched over with canes—all swelling the street, jockeying for limited space, sideswiping and barely missing the patrons occupying the outdoor Partisan-type cafes. The majority of the cafe habitues were wrinkled old men with Old Testament beards draped in their long white jelabus robes, sipping coffee black as coal.

Doug led Jack down a series of impossibly narrow, winding alleyways—turning left, then right—and soon Harry realized he would never know how to get out of here by himself.

"Doug," he asked, "Where the hell are we going?"

"We're almost there. You're gonna love this."

Moments later, they entered a small deserted courtyard with a statue of a Moroccan warrior on horseback dominating the center of the plaza. A series of pathways branched out from the statue, like spokes on a wheel. Harry followed Doug as he turned right down one of the darkened alleyways before stopping at a black cloth curtain draped over an archway. Doug parted the curtain and the two men walked in.

Harry was temporarily blinded by the darkness, but his eyes adjusted enough to discern a tiny alcove with several printed cushions lying on the floor. A skinny, haggard man with sunken cheeks sporting a straggly beard sat stoned-faced on an upturned barrel in front of a brown wooden door adorned with black wrought-iron engravings.

"Afternoon, Hamza!" Doug exclaimed casually, as if he was walking into the Las Vegas Hilton.

"Ah, *Labaas, bba ali* Sterris," the man said, peering through the gloom with lazy, half-mast eyes. "Nice to see you again. How's business?"

"Never better. This is my friend, Harry Miller from America. He's come to sample some of your fine commodities and visit with Zineb."

Hamza alertly sprang up, shaking Harry's hand. "Welcome my friend. What do you Americans say? Ah yes...any friend of Mr. Sterris is a friend of mine. Welcome to our country."

"Thank you. It's nice to be here."

"Come this way."

Hamza grabbed a key the size of a football hanging from a nearby hook. He opened the heavy brown door, ushering them into another murky black room emitting a strange smell, as if incense was burning close to hamburger on a grill. It was a larger room furnished with makeshift wooden benches and more cushions and pillows littering the floor. From hidden speakers, haunting, hypnotic trance rhythms resonated from an acoustic guitar. It reminded Harry of the flamenco-style strumming in Spanish folk music. Through the gloaming, Harry spotted four bodies lying prone, either on their backs or on their sides. Out of blackened shadows, flickering tiny red circles of light glimmered from intricately crafted oil lamps. The air was thick and heavy with what, Harry surmised, could only be opium smoke.

"Ready to get high?" asked Doug.

Harry said, "Damn right."

Doug walked over to another rail-thin hollow-eyed man squatting legs akimbo on an oriental rug.

"How ya doin," Imane!" cried Doug, slipping money into his open palm.

Imane reached around and picked up a chipped and cracked wooden box, extracting a soft black square wrapped in cellophane. He unwrapped the dark, sticky substance, and then placed it on a tray containing two sharp knives, a pair of scissors, a box of matches, and a small bowl resembling a doorknob attached to a long stem by means of a metal fitting. An oil lamp rested on the table. From a nearby shelf he grabbed a long, bamboo opium pipe. Harry had smoked opium a few times, but never with an opium pipe and oil lamp.

Imane struck a match and lit the oil lamp, picked up a small wad of opium, trimming the edges with scissors until he was left with a pea-size morsel. He placed the opium in the pipe-bowl, and held it over the oil lamp. Imane motioned Harry to lie on his side, and then handed him the pipe. Soon a stream of heat rose from the "chimney" of the oil lamp.

Harry sucked in the intoxicating vapors, trying to figure out what it smelled like; it seemed sickly-sweet and earthy at the same time with a perfume undertone from unknown flowers. As the pipe bubbled, Harry sucked in as much vapor as his lungs could stand. Then he handed the pipe to Doug lying prone next to him, a Cheshire cat grin plastered on his face.

At some point, nothing seemed to matter. Harry's worries, doubts, and problems melted away in a dream-like reverie, as if God was cleansing his soul, washing away every trace of anxiety twisting inside of him.

Breathtakingly high, orgasmic sensations coursed through his body as if a load of heroin boosted from his toes was shooting up to explode in his brain. In the corner, faint shadows from soft-colored amber and pink lamps danced on the walls like jittery stick figures. A dim blue light flickered from the ceiling. Dense, florid aroma from the pipe mingled with muted colors in the room creating an atmosphere as beautiful as an exotic garden. Music was still playing; Harry listened. Closing his eyes, he *felt* the music materializing from the speakers, *smelled* the colors of the blue light, *heard* the aroma of the unknown flowers in the garden. Opening his eyes, he *saw* the music cascading in waves before him like a gentle marine waterfall.

Harry and Doug Doug continued lying side-by-side, wordlessly. Time melting away like one of Dali's golden watches.

At some point, Doug sat up, languidly staring into space. He turned, gazing at Harry, whispering, "You know God..."

"What?"

"God."

"God?"

"Yeah...God."

"What about him?"

"If He made anything better..."

"Yeah...?"

"He kept it for himself..."

"Humm...right..."

Time passed. Doug spoke again...

"Jineb,"

"What..?"

"We need to see Jineb."

"Who is he?"

"He's...strange..."

As if weightless in a spaceship, Doug rolled over, struggling to lift himself. Then he reached over and pulled up Harry whose legs had morphed into two rubber hoses.

"Come on," Doug urged, "Let's see Imane."

The two men shambled over to where Imane was sitting in front of a black curtain. Doug slipped Imane more money and Imane parted the curtains. They entered the dark and smokey room. Harry spotted a single body lying sideways on a flat board, an opium pipe placed directly in front of his mouth.

"This is Jineb?" asked Harry.

Doug said, "Yes, he's flat."

"What?"

"Look at him. He's flat."

Harry edged closer, closer, peering through a dense layer of whitish yellow smoke. The top third of the gaunt figure was emaciated and rawboned, revealing tiny thin muscles barely visible beneath the skin. The lower two-thirds of his body was shockingly cadaverous, rubbery, dough-like flesh splayed out on the board with rippling layers rolling down from him as if he was melting.

"What the---?"

"He rarely gets up," said Doug. "He's laid there so long his muscles have atrophied."

Harry leaned forward, staring at two cavernous black holes submersed in a pallid skeleton with a thin covering of yellow skin. His mouth forming an "O" similar to the horrified man in the "The Scream" painting.

"Does he talk?" Harry asked, feeling uneasy, as if referring to a specimen in a jar.

"No," said, Imane. "He doesn't talk. He doesn't know his name. He doesn't know how old he is."

"Where did he come from?"

"No one knows. He was here when I came, and nobody remembers who he is."

Harry's stomach churned. "But...how did he get flat? You say he never gets up? I mean you have to get up sometime, right?..."

"Not really," said Iman. "I take care of him, feed him, give him water. He survives by charging people like you to see him."

"Christ, Iman," said Harry. "The guy has to go to the bathroom."

Iman grinned sheepishly. "Well, my friend, once in a while, but don't forget---"

"What?"

"Opium makes you constipated."

After Harry and Doug left the flat man, they walked a couple blocks to an outdoor cafe in Old Medina, woozy and lightheaded from the effects of the opium. As they waited for their espressos Doug asked, "So what did you think?"

"It's one of the craziest things I've ever seen."

"I feel a little guilty about showing him to you."

"Why?"

"I don't know. There's something about paying money to see freaks that freaks *me* out."

"I know what you mean. Do you think he's happy?"

"Happy? He's a fucking vegetable."

"I know, but what's his biggest worry?"

"Worries? He doesn't even know his own name."

"But, a lot of poets and writers used opium...like De Quincey... Coleridge...Baudelaire."

"So, what are you saying? That guy was no writer or poet—he was a mindless vegetable."

"Baudelaire called opium an artificial paradise."

"Come on, Harry. What are you driving at?"

"I'm going to stick around for a while."

"Where?"

"Back there."

"Back there? Back there! At the opium den?"

"Why not? I could use a few worry-free, mindless days."

"Jesus, Harry, are you serious? What about your life, your plans for the future? You want to stop dead in your tracks and waste your time in an opium den? What happens if you get so addicted that you wind up like poor Jineb? You'll get so far down, you'll never get out."

"I know Doug, but maybe the way down *is* the way out."

# Birth of the Cool

In the darkening night, Troy Littleton plodded along the sidewalk, the wind swirling all around him blowing snowflakes in his face. As the steady snow powdered the streets with a thin layer, he pulled his overcoat tighter around his body, crossing his arms, bending forward against the power of the gale force winds.

He was on his way to coach Osa Martin's house. He tugged his wool toboggan hat down over his forehead, leaving just enough room to see the sidewalk in front of him. Tiny specks of ice were already sticking to the front of his hat, and his hands were stiffening from the cold. As he was shivering past one of the maple trees lining the street, he heard a strange voice bellowing out, "That you, Troy Littleton?"

He instinctively jumped back, losing his balance, staggering to the other side of the sidewalk. From a crouching position, he peered over at the tree, unable to see anything. He began to slowly slink away.

"Wait, Troy!" the voice cried. "Don't be scared! It's only me—ole Rufus! You remember me! I saw you last summer."

Troy took a few steps towards the tree. There was something familiar about the man's voice. Then he remembered Rufus Johnson. He was a harmless old drunk he first met sitting on a lawn chair, drinking warm Colt 45. He cautiously approached the ghostly figure huddled under a tree. Gradually, he was able to make out the dim figure of Rufus sitting in the same broken-down lawn chair. Troy inched closer, realizing he was dressed exactly the same in tattered overalls and a beat-up fedora full of holes. A bottle of Colt 45 rested on the ground beside the chair. His only other protection from the elements was a wool blanket wrapped around him, but this too was full of holes.

"Rufus?"

"You bet it's ole Rufus! Come here, Troy! I hear you're just about the best darn young baseball player in the state of New York! Bats left, throws left, pitches like Warren Spahn, got a batting eye like an eagle, and runs like Willie Mays himself. Come here, Troy and say hello to ole Rufus!"

Troy shambled towards Rufus, taking off his toboggan hat, and flicking off the ice and snow, slapping it against his left leg as if it was baseball cap.

"Hi, Rufus. Isn't it kinda cold and snowy for you to be out here?"

"Don't you worry about ole Rufus, Troy. This weather ain't nuthin'. You shoulda seen the winter of '48. Damn blizzard every day, and no shelter anywhere for Rufus. I lived in a cardboard box for three freezing months. Hell, this ain't nuthin,' I tell ya."

Troy figured Rufus was homeless, and probably had not enjoyed the security and pleasures of a real home in a long time. He couldn't help but like the old guy. He had an engaging personality, and Troy had the feeling there were plenty of fascinating episodes in the man's life. He had certainly been around—where, Troy didn't know, but it seemed as if the old-timer had traveled many a hard road and seen things that he could only imagine.

"Well, Rufus, it's very cold out here, and it might get worse. Don't you want to go inside someplace?"

"Hell, no! You go inside someplace and right away they wanna start puttin' rules on you, tryin' to civilize you, makin' you hide your liquor, make your bed    treat you like you was a kid or somethin'. Better off here. Nobody tells ole Rufus what to do."

"Okay, I was just suggesting—"

"Wanna sip of my brew?"

"No thanks. I'm not much of a drinker."

"Well, I am!" cried Rufus, tilting the bottle to his lips, taking a long pull, and wiping his mouth with his tattered sleeve.

Troy laughed. "I can see that, Rufus. You sure enjoy your beer."

"Ain't beer, son. Malt liquor. Beer's too damn thin and watery. Hey, where you goin', anyway? Too damn cold out here for younguns."

"I'm going to coach Martin's house. You remember, he's my Little League coach."

"Oh, yes! The Mighty Man hisself. Best damn coach in the state."

"Didn't you tell me last summer he played professional ball somewhere?"

"Troy, I know you ain't dumb. You look kinda dumb to me, but you's a smart youngster. I told you about Osa Martin being one of the finest Negro League players I ever seen—and I seen 'em *all*. Satchel Paige, Smokey Joe Williams, Buck O'Neil—all of 'em."

"Rufus, tell me again. Who did Mr. Martin play for?"

"I told you, son. The Pittsburgh Crawfords!"

"Right! The Crawfords! I remember now!"

"Maybe you ain't so dumb."

"You said he was great, but he stopped playing, right?"

"Yes, that's what I said—and I told you not to tell anybody. You never told anybody, did you?"

"No, sir. I never told a soul."

"Well, you keep it between you and me."

"But I don't understand, Rufus. Why can't I say something? I think it's great that he was a terrific player and all. People in town should know about it."

"Now, Troy, you is a good kid. I like you. But there are some things that need keeping quiet. You understand me?"

"Yes, sir."

"Did you say you were headed for Mr. Martin's house right now?"

"Yes, sir."

"You been to his house before?"

"Yes, sir."

"He ever mention the Pittsburgh Craws?"

"No, sir."

"Why you going over there?"

"Well, I've been having some problems, and Mr. Martin is giving me some real good advice. I don't have a father at home and, well, he's been helping me out."

"Couldn't find a better man. Osa Martin is one of the finest men I ever met. Maybe you're a smart kid after all."

"Do you think I could ask him about his baseball career? It's only the two of us, and I'd like to hear it from him. You said he quit playing after just a couple years?"

"That's right."

"But you're not going to tell me why he quit, are you?"

"No, I'm not. If Osa wants to tell you, he will. If he don't, he won't. Simple as that."

"Do you think it would be okay for me to ask him?"

Rufus hesitated for a second, placing his hand on his chin. "I don't think he would mind you asking, Troy. Osa is a very private man, but if he likes you and trusts you, he might open up to you. Might do him some good. It's not a good thing to keep everything bottled up inside of you. Turns your guts sour. Might do some good. Never know in this world. You say Osa Martin is helping you out with some problems?"

"Yes, sir."

"Might work the other way, son."

"What do you mean?"

"Maybe you can help him out with some of his."

"I don't know about that. Listen Rufus, I better get going. It's getting late, and the snow seems to be picking up. I don't want to come home in a blizzard."

"Can't blame you there, son. Sure you don't want a slug? Warm your bones!"

"No thanks. I hope to see you again sometime."

"Well, son, you never can tell. One thing about life. You never can tell. You take care, now—and keep playing baseball for as long as you can. There ain't nuthin' better in a boy's life—or a man's life either, for that matter."

Troy waved good-bye, twisting around one more time to see Rufus taking another swig from his bottle and brushing snow away from his face. Trudging doggedly through the thickening snow, he arrived at Mr. Martin's house. Once again, he walked up the steps, knocked on the door, and waited for his coach.

Opening the door, Osa Martin cried, "Well, look who it is! The next player to hit .400 in the majors!"

"Hi, Mr. Martin. Is it okay to come in?"

"Of course! I was expecting you! Come in! Come in!"

Troy entered the house, removed his overcoat, shook off the snow, and handed his coat to Mr. Martin who hung it up in a closet next to a roaring fireplace.

"Come on over by the fire, son. It's a lot warmer over here!"

Troy ambled across the room, sat down in his usual chair, gazing at the flickering red and yellow flames. Osa walked into the kitchen and momentarily returned with a Royal Crown soda in his hand. "You're a Royal Crown man, right?"

"Yes, sir!"

"So how's it going?" asked Osa, taking a seat across from Troy.

"Oh, fine. My mother is going out with a new man."

"That sounds wonderful. What's he like? Do you like him?"

"Oh, he's a real swell guy! He's a lawyer in Philadelphia, and he brought us some ice cream and some rock 'n roll records!

"That *is* good news. I'm sure your mother is very pleased."

"She's like a changed person. She even smiles sometimes."

Osa laughed good-naturedly. "Well, *that's* certainly good to hear."

Troy faced the robust fire, staring at the lively, jumping flames as if answers to his problems could be found smoldering in the burning embers. "Mr. Martin, I've been thinking about what you said about me trying to be perfect at everything."

"Yes."

"And you're right. I never realized it, but I really need to be perfect or the best at everything, and if I'm not, I quit—like marbles and kick soccer."

"So how do you feel about that?"

"I feel, like, terrible… stupid."

"Why?"

"Because I know in my heart it's not possible, but I try anyway, and I get just… paralyzed."

"Paralyzed?"

"Well, maybe that's not the right word. I get tense all over. M y mother calls them panic attacks."

"You get nervous."

"Right! I feel very uncomfortable, and I want to jump out of my skin."

"Well, Troy, trying to be perfect is basically attempting to do something well, and that's okay. But when your goal is not to make mistakes, you're going off in the wrong direction. You can try to be flawless pursuing a particular goal like a test at school, but it is not a good idea as a philosophy of life."

"Why not?"

"Because we, as humans, are part of nature, and nature isn't meant to be perfect. You can say a machine can be perfect, but we are not machines. In fact, thinking of nature as perfect would ruin its beauty. Can you imagine saying, "Wow, that rainbow would be perfect if the blue was only brighter."

"I see..."

"We should all live in the moment and forget about the goal of perfection. It gets in the way of wonderment and appreciation."

"Gosh, Mr. Martin, how did you get so smart?"

Osa chuckled. "Well, it helps to be older. Hopefully, we get wiser as we grow older."

"I guess I have some learning to do."

"Well, you're got plenty of time. You just need to relax and be satisfied with who you are, and not rely too much on imaginary judgments from other people."

"What do you mean?"

"When someone strives for perfection, they are really saying, 'I'm not good enough just as I am,' and these feelings come from thinking you have to live up to an unrealistic goal—like being perfect."

"Does that mean I'm insecure?"

"It could lead to insecurity, if you keep giving other people this power to judge you."

Osa stood up from his chair and walked over to a small cherry cabinet with glass doors and took out a bottle of Hennessy brandy. He grabbed a glass from the shelf and poured himself a drink, and then returned to the chair. Glancing around the room, Troy's eyes resting an album he had seen before, one with a shadowy black man playing the trumpet on the cover.

"Say, Mr. Martin, what's that album over there? The one propped up next to the record player on top of the bookcase."

Osa sipped his brandy. "That's a classic record by a jazz musician named Miles Davis. He plays the trumpet, and he has a great band backing him up. The album is called *Birth of the Cool*."

"Wow. That's a cool title."

"It's a cool album. Do you want to hear it?"

"Sure!"

Osa strode over to the top shelf of the bookcase and placed the album on the turntable and hit a switch. The arm swung over, dropping the needle down on the record. Soon Troy heard a strange, captivating sound he had never heard before. He only knew rock 'n roll and a little country music. He had never heard jazz. He lay back in his chair, mesmerized by the beauty of the melody, powerful and beautiful, as if it was emanating from another universe, timeless and profound. He tried to figure out what other instruments were playing, He thought he heard a saxophone solo, and there was definitely a piano and drums. When the side of the album ended, Troy straightened up in his chair.

"Gee, Mr. Martin. I never heard anything so beautiful in my life. It's like he's playing from a place I never knew existed—like someplace where great spirits are celebrating life."

Osa nodded. "That's a good way to put it, Troy. Jazz is the music of soul. It's like a soulful community of spirits where harmony and splendor come together.

You know Troy, learning about jazz may help you with some of your problems."

"Really?"

"Well, jazz is all about free form and changing the tempo according to your mood and the mood of the audience. For the most part, it's not written down like classical music. In other words, it's almost the opposite of trying to be perfect and play the same song the same way every time. It's about mood changes and improvisation. It's also about living in the present without distracting thoughts like trying to be perfect."

Troy leaned back in the recliner, anxious for Mr. Martin to play the other side of the record. Listening to the music made him feel closer to his coach. He wanted to know more about his life.

"Mr. Martin, do you know an old man named Rufus in town? I think he's probably homeless. I have run into him a couple times."

Osa paused before taking another sip of brandy. "Yes, I have known Rufus for a long time. He was a scout for the old Negro Leagues a long time ago. He's a very odd person, but he's remarkably intelligent and knows the game of baseball inside and out. He discovered many excellent prospects in the old days, including me."

"Well, I don't know how to say this, but Rufus told me you were a great baseball player and you had a funny nickname—Might Man. Is that true? Do you want to tell me about it? And please don't think I'm prying into your life! You don't have to tell me anything—really, Mr. Martin!"

"It's okay, Troy I don't mind telling you, but it's a rather long story. Are you sure you want to hear a long story?"

"Yes, sir."

"Well, feel free to close your eyes and relax in the warmth of the fire. I'm going to tell you the whole story. And by the way, I have never told this story to anyone."

Jackie closed his eyes; Osa began to speak:

"I was playing for the Pittsburgh Crawfords in 1934. The fans called us the Craws. We had just won the most games of any team in the Negro Leagues and fielded a great team composed of some of the greatest players in the Negro Leagues. We felt we were good enough to beat any of the white major-league teams, but of course we never got the chance. I played right field, because I had a strong arm and could make that long throw from right field to third base. Later on, Satchel Paige told me that I played just like Roberto Clemente. I was in my second year. I batted .325 the first year and .376 in 1934. That was when I got the nickname 'Mighty Man.' A really good pitcher named 'Cannonball' Willis gave me that name after I hit two home runs in a game in St. Louis. I hit twelve home runs my first year, and then in 1934 I hit fifteen—just one shy of Josh Gibson. So my career was really taking off, and after the season was over, the owner, Gus Greenlee, took me to the Crawford Grill, one of Pittsburgh's favorite night spots, and we listened to a young singer named Lena Horne that night. That woman could sing like an angel... Anyway, Mr. Greenlee told me that I was going to get a nice, fat contract for the coming year, and he said, in a joking manner, to go out and get me a fancy Packard automobile...

"After the season was over, we went barnstorming across the country in a cramped, sweltering hot bus, playing other touring teams or local teams they would put together. In those days, even the big white stars like Babe Ruth, Dizzy Dean, and Bob Feller would barnstorm in the off season to keep in shape or make some extra money. One time we played a white team in Mississippi, and Babe Ruth was in right field. Obviously, I had heard about Ruth, but seeing him in person was something else. He was what you call bigger than life. I think he hit two home runs, and boy, one of them was the longest home run I ever saw. He was quite a guy too. He was one of the few white players who would socialize with us, and he even came to some of our clubs at night. That Babe sure loved his cigars, women, and alcohol…

"Anyway, back then the black players—and every black person, really—lived in a parallel universe. We didn't have any entries into the white world. There were segregation laws all over the South called Jim Crow laws, and everything was separate; and believe me, they were definitely not equal. A lot of times we slept on the bus, went hungry because restaurants wouldn't serve us, so we'd go to the black section of town. Sometimes, we'd pull over and pick fruit from a field, and one time in Alabama, we ate sardines out of a Bell Fruit jar from a kettle fired up in someone's backyard. Since we couldn't congregate in the white world, black folks built their own social networks. We had our own churches, restaurants, schools—everything a community needs, although we were much more destitute. Also, we came across a lot of mean people who just hated us simply because of the color of our skin. But they loved to watch us play because we were so good, and we also entertained the crowds…

"We played a different brand of baseball—much flashier, bolder, and much more exciting than in the majors. We ran the bases like our uniforms were on fire. And the pitchers would throw any kind of pitch they wanted, like spitters, shine balls, cut balls, balls soaked with tobacco juice—anything. Everything and anything was legal—even spiking players with your sharpened cleats! And they'd throw at your head as soon as look at you—just to announce their arrival. Satchel was, by far, the best entertainer. Sometimes, he'd clown around and pitch from his knees. One time he made the catcher sit in a rocker chair, his control was so good. Other times, he ran to third base instead of first. Another time, he pitched from second base—and still struck out batters! He was something else. I used to say that if Satchel was white, he'd be a millionaire. I want to be clear about this, Troy. Sure, we entertained white people, but we never compromised our manhood or our dignity. If we thought they were just laughing at us and not with us, then we'd get serious and beat them by twenty-five runs. We also made fun of them, using code names for words like *cracker* and *redneck…*

"Now, besides the usual community places, we also went to what we would call 'the other side of the tracks.' Well, I can't be too specific, but there are certain kinds of illicit pleasures that young men do that are not very nice but very tempting… Remember, there were a lot of lynchings of black people down in the South; it was a very dangerous place, especially at night in an unknown town.

"Well, I was barnstorming with the Craws in late November. We played a tough Negro League team called the Alabama Black Barons. I think Willie Mays played for this team later on. Well, we won the game, and later that night we all went across the tracks to what they called a juke house or juke joint. These were small clapboard houses along the side of the road that served beer and whiskey, and they usually had a blues player singing on the premises. There was also gambling, mostly dice games like craps or card games like bid whist. We were in the tiny town of Chickasaw, Alabama, just a few miles north of Mobile. It was Josh Gibson's idea to check out Posey's Juke House just on the outskirts of town. All of us were a little apprehensive about this place, because we didn't know anyone and these places can be very rough, if you know what I mean. It wasn't just white folks killing black folks. We also killed plenty of each other. I'll tell you how rough they were. They only served beer in paper cups, and you could only drink whiskey out of the bottle. They couldn't use any ceramic mugs or beer glasses, because the men would tear each other up, cutting and stabbing and blood flying all over the place…

"It was Satchel, Josh Gibson, Rap Dixon, myself, and a player named Wee Willie Johnson who went into Posey's around midnight. Things were just getting started. It was a dark place. Very simple furniture. A couple of small pine tables and chairs and just a plain wooden bar with some whiskey bottles behind the counter. When I first came in I heard a blues singer who was practically hidden in the corner sitting on a cane-bottomed chair. I had never heard a voice like that before. It was very emotional and heartbreaking—a very powerful wailing, like he was some kind of tortured soul. No one was paying much attention to him. He had an acoustic guitar and a bottle of whiskey by his side. We grabbed a table in the middle of the room, and a fine-looking waitress came over to take our order. We all ordered beer and a bottle of whiskey to share. Well, it turned out we had nothing to fear, because one of the patrons who was in a corner shooting craps looked up at us and screamed, 'There's Satchel!' Well, the whole place just exploded with good vibes. Everybody loved Satchel, and then they started buying us drinks, and the blues player caught the spirit and started playing more upbeat dancing songs. I remember one of them sounded like an old ragtime jump song about hot tamales being red hot. The guy was just mesmerizing...

"So the people started getting more excited, shouting and dancing, and then all of a sudden the blues singer stood up like a rock 'n' roll singer—like Elvis—and he began to sing and shake and whirl around the whole place. We were having a great time, and then this cute girl in a plain cotton dress came up to me. She was a white girl—the only one in the place. Someone told me later that she was the farm owner's daughter, but she couldn't have been more than twenty-one years old. She was well-built, with reddish hair and a charming smile that could make your heart melt. Anyway, she seemed interested in me, and we had a few drinks. Then, after a while, she asked me to go back to her place. By this time I was—well, Troy truthfully, I was drunk. I said yes, and we left the house and went to her car—a beautiful, brand new Ford coup. She got in and drove for a while. I don't remember how long, but I remember looking out the car window and seeing steel girding, and I realized we were on a bridge, but I still didn't know where she was taking me. We crossed the bridge and traveled a few miles, and I saw a sign that said Pascagoula River State Wildlife Area. Apparently, we were in a national park surrounded by woods and fields. I never did see a river. Anyway, the girl pulled over and said something like, 'This looks like a good spot.' We were what you kids call making out when I looked up from the seat and the harsh beam from a flashlight blinded my eyes. It was a cop, and he was none too happy. He made us get out of the car and asked a bunch of questions, like who we were and where we were going, and he particularly wanted to know how old the girl was and where she was from. The girl told him she was twenty years old, but I don't think he believed her. After interrogating us for awhile, he told the girl to get in her car and go home. He told me to get in the back of the police car. We rode for a few miles, and I asked him what I was being arrested for. He said, 'The Mann Act,' as if I would know what that was. I said I never heard of a Mann Act, and he said,

'Too bad for you.' When we got to the police station, it was the first time I realized I wasn't in the state of Alabama. I was in Mississippi, and we had crossed the Mississippi River. I had no idea, but I was in big trouble. The Mann Act makes it a crime to take a woman across state lines for immoral proposes, and if she's underage or a prostitute, you're in real trouble. Well, to make a long story *longer*, I was sent to jail for five years—Parchment Farm in Mississippi, the worst prison on the face of the earth. I can't tell you how brutal the guards were. I saw many men injured and killed by either the guards or fellow prisoners. I picked cotton for ten hours a day, six days a week, and the guards constantly lashed my back with a thick leather strap called Black Annie. I still have the red marks to this day.

"My boss, Mr. Greenlee, was outraged and hired a big-time lawyer from New York to take my case and work on getting me released. Well, the lawyer was successful, but it took three years, and by then I was worn out from the back-breaking work, lack of sleep, and terrible food. Mr. Greenlee gave me another tryout, but it seemed my body had suffered too much abuse. So that was when I hung up my spikes. After that, I wanted to get far away from the South and Midwest, so I came to New York state...

"So that's what Rufus was talking about when he told you I was nicknamed Mighty Man. And also why I suddenly disappeared from the world of baseball. But I have no regrets. There were many other players who never got the chance to play in the majors because of the color of their skin, the war, or unexpected injuries. You need talent to make it as a professional player, but a little luck doesn't hurt either. I guess my luck wasn't so good, but I don't blame anyone but myself. I should have never gone to that juke joint and certainly never left with that strange girl. Those were dangerous times and I was young, naive, and pretty stupid. So, Troy, don't make any similar mistakes. Some of these temptations like drinking, gambling, and women can be a pretty powerful draw on a young person, but you must keep your eyes on the prize, and the prize is not just becoming the best baseball player you can, but also becoming the best person. You can't let these other things distract you from your future goals, whatever they may be."

Osa paused. He looked at Troy still sitting with his eyes closed. He wondered if he had put the boy to sleep. Then, Troy opened his eyes.

"Mr. Martin, that was the best—and saddest—story I ever heard. I couldn't imagine spending three years in a horrible jail, getting whipped with a black belt. And you missed out on a chance to be a major leaguer. Golly, I guess you wish you could have done things differently."

"I don't know. From where I'm sitting right now, I wouldn't change a thing."

"You mean you're not bitter about the way you were treated?"

Osa paused, glancing at the mantelpiece. "Well, in life you really have no choice. You need to take the good with the bad and count your blessings every day. Troy, it's time for you to get back home. It's late, and it's snowing harder outside. Do you want me to drive you home?"

"Oh no, Mr. Martin! I love to walk in the snow—and I've got a lot to think about! I'm so glad you told me about what happened during your baseball career—even if there were a lot of bad people in your life. It's fascinating—and I won't tell anybody!"

"It's okay, Jackie. You can tell people. You can't run from your past. I just prefer to keep it to myself. It's no big secret."

"Well, I think you had the most wonderful, exciting experiences, and I wish I could have seen you play! Could you really throw harder than Roberto Clemente?"

"Well, that's what Rufus says."

"And Rufus is never wrong!"

"Right," said Osa, smiling. "Now, you get along. I'll see you next week, if you want to come by."

"Can I? I'm not being a pest, am I?"

"Not at all, Troy. I'll see you next Monday, same time."

"Sounds great!"

"Oh, Jackie! Hold on! You forgot something."

"What?"

Osa went to the record player, grabbed the album, came back, and handed it to Troy. "Here you are, Troy. A gift from me to you.'"

"Thanks, Mr. Martin. I'll take real good care of it."

"No problem. Watch your step going home."

Osa watched Troy until he disappeared into the darkness of the night. He closed the door, walked over to the coffee table, and picked up his glass of brandy. Then he stood in front of the fireplace, his head bowed, watching the flames burning intensely. His eyes drifted slowly upward to one of the pictures on the mantelpiece, gazed at it for a moment before lifting his glass, and downing the rest of his drink.

# Grayson and Mr. Defoe

Grayson Pepperdine sat in a brown leather club chair in the living room of his parent's house in Muncie, Indiana. He was drinking a Budweiser gazing impassively out a canted bay window at the isolated street in front of him. Somehow in his absence the old familiar neighborhood growing up had changed into strange and uncomfortable place to be. In the past two hours he had not seen a single person or vehicle of any kind. He wondered why the familiar environs outside the window were oddly sterile and abnormally hygienic, emitting antiseptic odors of chlorine and household disinfectants through a crack in one of the bay windows. He tried to locate something different, something out of the ordinary, but as he mechanically rotated his head from left to right, all he could see were pastel, bleached-out cookie cutter houses landscaped with identical, synthetic AstroTurf lawns speckled with perfectly trimmed pale green bushes. He could not see any discernible signs of movement anywhere, not even a random slip of paper floating in the breeze. He wondered what happened to the wholesome Disney images of his childhood.

Grayson closed his eyes. He was tired of trying to figure what was real and what was an illusion. He was beginning to doubt his ability to tell the difference, and figured it did not matter much anyway. Opening his eyes, he peered out the window once more. Nothing had changed. Omnipresent melancholy inertness hovered over the neighborhood like humidity with a broken heart. He wanted to detect a hint of life, like a bird flying past him or the postman delivering the mail. There was also something peculiar about maple streets lining both sides of the street. They looked like faded, leafless one-dimensional cardboard cutouts. He guessed the leaves had probably fallen off, but then he realized there were no leaves on the ground. *Shouldn't there be some kids raking leaves, piling them up by the sidewalk so*

the city could haul them away? Isn't that what I did when I was a kid? I used
to love to run and jump into a big pile of leaves and bury myself in my own
musty brown cave.

His thoughts about the mystery of the maple trees soon drifted away,
replaced by a more serious concern. He wondered if the whole town had
become transformed into a ghostly theme park that never attracted any
tourists. The only thing he looked forward to everyday was waving to the
paperboy as he rode past on his bicycle flipping the newspaper on the lawn.

Grayson reached into his pocket and retrieved the vial containing
Little Freddy's mysterious acid. He popped one in his mouth, thinking:
*In the past few weeks I have started hearing strange voices. Well, not exactly
voices, but the voice of a real person. Oops, there's another small problem.
This person is dead. Why is Daniel Defoe talking to me? Just because I read
his stupid book? Was Muncie anything like London four hundred years ago? I
doubt it. As far as I know old London smelled like an outhouse baking in the
sun showering piss and excrement down on the city—a literal shit storm---"*

*Grayson..*

"What? Is that you Mr. Defoe? Are you awake? I thought you only
spoke to me at night."

*Grayson, I'm always awake.*

"Great. You want a sleeping pill?"

*I want to remind you. Did you forget?*

"No, I didn't forget."

*'Tis an ill time to be sick in.*

"Mr. Defoe, I remember."

*This plague has happened before Grayson. In England, if someone
complained of a solitary ailment, the terrified villagers immediately assumed
they had contracted the plague. In the early days of the dire pestilence,
commonplace faces were strangely altered, becoming harsh and grotesque as
malevolent transfigurations occurred throughout the dying city. Even the
faded gray portentous monuments appeared more sinister and imposing than
usual, like ancient fortresses built above the foggy Scottish lowlands to ward
off invading English armies. An entire community in the midst of a horrible
imperceptible virus, ominous black clouds hovering over the land, casting
gloom and darkness on every living thing---*

"Grayson! What are you doing?"

"Wha---!" Grayson practically jumping out of his seat. He didn't hear his mother's footsteps approaching, and her piercing authoritarian voice sent shock waves shuddering through his body. He turned sideways, glanced up, and saw her standing there with her hands on her hips expecting an answer. Instinctively, he looked down, averting her eyes.

"Oh, sorry mother. I was just sitting here...uh, waiting for the paperboy."

*On the outskirts of town, the Black Death was dwelling in the killing fields, lying in wait for those souls with vile blood coursing through their veins, victims of dead-like phantoms of godless affliction.*

"Is that it? Just sitting there?" asked his mother.

*A small boy, lost and confused, wandered in the country gazing upon multitudes of strange and prophetic sights and sounds. He looked and saw prehistoric wino beggars huddled in soiled newspapers, freezing in the bowels of filthy city sewers; wild-haired, wicked---*

"Well, no. I am waiting for the paperboy to ride by."

*Old wrinkled crones dancing in spidery graveyards, cursing the moon and worshiping Neolithic gods; ragged orphan children with smudgy faces begging for crumbs in a homeless gypsy park; muddy, disheveled young nymphs---*

"What for?"

*In lotus-eating poppy fields damned with curses and addiction; drunken circus---*

"I just want to see some sign of life—somebody moving out there. Besides, father needs the paper, right?"

*Clowns, court jesters lurching recklessly down Cathedral Street with big red noses and floppy hats; skinless zombies fornicating on dirty, urine-stained mattresses---*

"Grayson, you must have something better to do than stare out a window all day. I don't mean to nag you or be a nuisance, but do you have any plans? I mean, you know...plans for the future."

Grayson lifted his head slightly, peering up at his mother as if he was six years old and just pissed his pants. Then he realized that even if he was fourteen years old and pissed his pants in church she still would not show any outwardly emotion. She was the ice-queen of emotional cautiousness, sober respectability, and middle class propriety. In his whole life Grayson had never heard his mother raise her voice out of frustration, or throw a prissy fit like every other mother in the country who had a fucked up kid and a lifeless android husband. As his chin slumped against his chest, he completely forgot the question she asked.

"Grayson please. Are you listening to me at all?"

Grayson glanced up at his mother. For a second he saw her face turn into a gray-green block of stone, possessing one eye—an evil satanic eye just like the weird one on the back of a dollar bill—the one isolated on the top of a granite pyramid. Then, she was back to her old self: composed, unemotional, and very unlikely to touch or hug another person. "Yes, of course. You were saying…"

"Your plans, Grayson. What are your plans?"

"Plans?"

"Yes, Grayson. What do you want to do with your life?"

"I want to be a famous photographer like Diane Arbus."

"Who?"

"She took pictures of these really weird people in New York City."

"All right. But, don't you think you should be doing something in the meantime?"

"Yes, of course. I'm going to check out some art classes at the community college."

"Really? You mean Ivy Tech?"

"Yes, Ivy Tech. They're teaching…cunnilingus."

"What is that? A new art style?

"Yes, it's very *avant-garde*."

"Okay, Grayson That's a good plan. Anything is better than staring out this window all day."

"Yes, ma'am."

"Your father will be home soon. You'd better get dressed for dinner. I'll be out in the kitchen if you need anything."

*Lonely pock-marked, gaped-tooth prostitutes peeking out from dusty drawn window shades. Suffering feudal wives wrapped in brown paper bags, hungry peasants broken on the wheel, oxen yokes collared on rusty necks, suffering grim determination. Grayson, in my travels I have encountered a few misguided souls who believed they saw apparitions in the air, heard murderous voices that never spoke, saw gruesome signs that never appeared. But then, I witnessed the imagination of the people turning inward, wayward and possessed. Locked in like criminals, they beheld things that were nothing but stale, fetid air.*

"Is that it? Mr. Defoe? Thanks for the gibberish. Please Danny, tell me why I am listening to a dead wacko from England who never wrote anything but Robinson Crusoe and Moll Flanders. And who the fuck reads Moll Flanders today?

*You do not have to be rude Grayson. I am trying to help you.*

"Fuck off, okay?"

Grayson waved his hand in the air as if to shoo Defoe away, and returned to gazing out the window for any sign of earthly existence. Finally, he saw his father turn in the driveway, and get out of his Buick sedan, the *Wall Street Journal* clutched firmly under his arm. Grayson followed him until he entered the front door. Suddenly, the paperboy rode by on his bike throwing the newspaper on the lawn. Smiling broadly, Grayson waved enthusiastically to the kid. The paperboy turned around and gave him the finger. Grayson laughed his ass off.

"Grayson?"

"What? Oh, mother, you took me by surprise."

"Are you coming to dinner?"

"Coming!"

Grayson lifted his head which felt like a half-filled water balloon with soupy brains sloshing inside. He pushed down with both hands and hoisted himself up. His legs wobbled uneasily as he walked into the dining room, spotting his father sitting at the head of the table wearing his shirt and tie from the office, calmly reading the newspaper. Grayson took a seat in the middle of the table. His father tossed the paper on the table, peering at him over the top of black horned-rim glasses perched on the bridge of his nose. The suspicious gaze made Grayson feel like a homeless tramp who sneaked in from the Hobo Jungle for a free meal. He wished they would feed him under the table like a dog. But he automatically assumed the rigid-spine position he was trained to do since childhood, folding his hands together on the table, mentally preparing for the silence to commence. The only sound in the room was coming from a fancy chandelier hanging from the ceiling, its tinkling crystals tapping lightly against one another. This silent ritual at the table unnerved Grayson to no end, and he never understood its meaning or purpose. *Did every family do this? Create a ghostly silence so all-consuming that you could actually hear someone swallow their food?* As usual, his father was the first one to speak.

"So, Grayson, what did you do all day?"

Even though stoned and crazy Grayson knew the obvious insinuation behind the question. He knew exactly what his father really wanted to say: *So, my worthless drug addict, pill-popping loser of a son, did you get off your lazy ass and look for a job today?*

"Well, dad. I didn't do much. I'm not feeling too great."

"Really? What's the matter?"

*I keep hearing the voice of some crazy guy from England warning me about a plague that's going to wipe out the whole world.*

"I don't know. It's nothing. Maybe an upset stomach. Maybe the food in Muncie doesn't agree with me."

Grayson's mother came trotting in from the kitchen carrying a freshly baked chicken resting in a white ceramic bowl. She set it down in the middle of the table, and took a seat facing her husband.

"Forrest, would you like to say grace?"

"Yes, Nancy. I'd be glad to."

"Our Heavenly Father, we come before you...

*Eerie animal noises from subterranean caves hungry, squealing flea-infested rats from London town in tenebrous alleys. I witnessed malodorous, smoke-filled bodegas where young people hunched together, wasting their life away. Eternal cries of human pain filled my ears and I begged for relief. I wonder when this plague will end and how many more lives the Black Death will wipe out? 'Tis a sorry tale indeed...*

"Amen."

"Amen."

"Amen."

"Nancy, the chicken looks terrific! You remind of that old commercial, 'My wife; I think I'll keep her.'"

"I hope so, Forrest. Who else would make you these divine meals?"

"Grayson was telling me he doesn't feel well."

"Oh, really? What's the matter?"

"Nothing, mother. Just an upset stomach."

"Well, you need to take better care of yourself and stick to a better diet. You eat too much junk food and sodas."

"Yes, mother."

*I do not understand these puerile agitations and strange indifferences to one's fellowman. The night before last a dead cart stopped at Brewster Hall and the transparent putrefying body of the town constable was brought down to the door very, very dead, and the buriers or bearers, as they were called, placed him gently into the creaky wooden cart wrapped only in a sacramental blanket, the color of dried blood…the stench of darkness…Black Death multiplying…even as they carried him away.*

"Uh…can I be excused?"

"Grayson, you haven't eaten a thing!"

"Sorry, mother. It's my stomach…"

"Okay, go to your room. I'll bring you some Alka-Seltzer in a little while."

"Thank you."

"Take it easy, son. Get some rest."

"Yes, father."

Grayson managed to stand up from the table, and staggered unevenly to his room. He closed the door, collapsed on the bed, and lay with his head propped on a pillow. Gazing at the ceiling fan rotating lazily above him for several minutes, he sensed the fan inching closer to him. At first he was not concerned, but suddenly he had a terrible flashback to "The Pit and the Pendulum." Bounding off the bed, he sprawled on the floor, clutching his stomach. Then he rolled over again, peeking at the fan. It was back to its original position.

"Mr Defoe?"

*Yes.*

"Can I make a plan for the future?"

*Yes.*

"I know the Black Death is coming and it's going to wipe out all of mankind, but I need a plan in the meantime."

*What do you want to do?*

"I really do not want to be a famous photographer like Diane Arbus. I want to track down all the people she photographed and see what happened to them."

*Why?*

78

"I don't know. It seems that they should not be forgotten, like somebody should write a journal about what happened to their lives."

*I think that's a good idea. Perhaps, you will find that they will be saved from the horrors of the Black Death.*

"Are they going to be saved?"

*I don't know. 'Tis an ill time to be sick in.*

# I Wouldn't Harm a Fly

DEAR DIARY

September 28:

*Call me Lori, the killer.*

*Lately, my memories are worthless recollections of woozy drunken nights in cheapass, beer-sodden dormitories, humping and sucking total fucking losers in cramped, creaking, bunk beds. I vaguely remember struggling to remove some stupid dumbass fratboy passed out on top of me, cursing my horrible fate. And yes, Dear Diary, through it all, loathing the messiness of sex, like the time I had to wipe sticky cum from my lips and chest with a dirty towel from a filthy bathroom.*

*Glancing down at the insignificant names, I try to connect at least one person with a meaningful moment. But they all blur together in an alcoholic, marijuana, Xanax haze. I run my fingers over the pages I have written, stopping at the name of Maury Gutherage. Who the fuck was he? Maybe I had sex with him on a beach somewhere, or went home with him after drinking all night at the Palms. Come to think of it, I must have been pretty hard up to sleep with some douchebag with a name like Maury.*

*I remember hearing faint, muffled sounds in the heat of a clammy, humid night, the haunting, soft murmur of a distant stereo, and wondering if the singer would approve of me having sex with some asshole while he was singing. One night, I stopped a guy right in the middle of sex and asked him to turn off Rod Stewart on the stereo. I can't have sex with anybody while "Maggie May" is playing.*

*Frankly, most of the time I remember very little about the evening. Yet there are other times when I can recall the weirdest, minutest details. Perhaps, he had a button missing on his shirt, or a tiny mole on his thigh, or a broken shoelace on his sneakers, or a red birthmark the shape of a butterfly. I remember different aromas, especially aftershaves and colognes like Halston, Fahrenheit, and Obsession, learning to stay away from losers who wore something cheap and tacky like Stetson.*

October 10:

*I have them listed pretty much in chronological order, but there's no way the timeline is remotely correct. If I don't write them down in a couple days it gets real tricky. Sometimes there is more than one in one night. Sometimes I can vividly picture their faces in the midst of extreme sexual pleasure. A few of these assholes would scream like ravaged beasts when they came inside of me. Other losers were the quiet, moaning type, perhaps calling out stupid names like Mommy, or My Little Pussy. Rarely did they share any love or tenderness. Oh, there's Barry Nelson's name. He was rough with me. He loved to tie my hands with his strong, athletic arms and pin me down on the bed. He would lean over me and yell obscenities like, Do you want it up the ass, bitch? I wonder if Barry Nelson will go to hell. He is certainly going to die before his time.*

*I can't find one guy I would be sorry to see end his life in a violent, painful death. Okay, there's Jason Jarvis with the asterisk, but I don't know what the asterisk means. Did I sleep with him? Maybe I got so drunk that I can't remember if we had sex. Actually, I have a mean crush on Jason, so I hope we didn't sleep together...but I can't be sure.*

October 18:

*Henry Dobson? Who the fuck was he? I hate the name Henry, maybe even more than Maury. I think he was a cute Pi Kappa Phi or maybe he was some steroid bonehead on the football team. I know he loved to stick his penis in my mouth until I started choking and coughing. Other times I would roll over on the bed and let him mount me doggy-style. I loved to prop my elbows on the pillows and lift my ass high into the air and offer myself as a kind of sacrificial gift for the Gods. Too bad he's the bastard who's going to be sacrificed.*

*Jesus, there's Doobie McDermott. How did he get on the list? Christ, everybody knows he's a faggy art major from New York City who probably*

81

*already has AIDS. He loved to perform oral sex on me and I always showered thoroughly before we went out. I wanted him to lick me as much as he wanted. I can picture him now kissing me, feeling me up, moving his lips from my mouth to my breast, twirling his tongue around my swollen, tingly nipples until I was eager and ready. He gave me many wonderful orgasms; I gave him a taste of death.*

*I know it's perverted to keep a record of all my conquests, but it really makes me feel better, spewing out this boatload of poisonous venom inside me. Why do my moods vacillate from self-absorption to self-loathing? Why this raging hatred of men? Can they all be scumbags? I am boiling with the wrath of a thousand demons. Let's face it, Miss Diary, my only hope is that they find a miracle cure for this deadly disease. And that's not likely—I'm going down way too fast. So, how long can I last at this rate? I am rapidly losing precious energy despite this repulsive medicine I have to take every four hours. God, my nights are horrible…unspeakable, like something out of an Edgar Allen Poe story. Tossing and turning. Cold sweats. Fuckin' low-grade flu.*

*Well, Dearest Diary, at least I'm keeping my weight down! I know you love that! I'd rather be dead than fat!*

*I wonder if Jason Jarvis is in love with me. I could be in love with him, but I'm not sure. I'm not sure what love feels like—nobody ever gave it to me, as far as I know. But, hey! I love someone who is really great!!! Me!!!!*

*Sorry about that last entry, Miss Diary. It was bullshit. Love me? Get-the-fuck. I want to rip my heart out. I want to slash a razor across my face. I want someone to hang me up by my toes and skin me alive. I should receive a blue ribbon for self-loathing. After all, I am special. Who the fuck hates themselves more than me? But, really. It's just crazy. I was always such a smart girl, and full of life and curiosity! God, I don't know. Well, maybe I know something. My father was cold-as-shit. You think a little girl could get a hug once in a while. Ah, forget it. I mean, it MUST be his fault, right? Who wouldn't like me? I am adorable. I am the cutest girl on campus. Really.*

October 24:

*I know this disease means I will never make it as an actress. It's such a shame. That's all I ever wanted to be. I wish there was a spotlight on me all the time, and I wish the only sounds I could hear in my head were sounds of an audience's applause. Maybe I can get an applause machine to place next to my bed. It's a start.*

November 6:

*Sadly, Miss Diary, my body is deteriorating. Damnit. I'm not sure how much longer I can keep up this phony pretense of normality. It's a good thing I'm a great actress. I can't believe these immature wingnuts can't see through my charade—especially my stupid roommates! I could turn into a rabbit and they wouldn't notice.*

November 14:

*I don't know how I will handle the decline of my wonderful good looks. How am I going to maintain my charming personality in the face of deterioration, disease, and death? Has anyone ever met a charming leper? I am not going down alone. You can be sure of that Dear Diary! Call me Satan's wife, doing a great service, bringing more wicked fornicators to the gates of Hell. Tonight, I counted my victims. Since I have become infected, I have amassed 18 names on my marvelous death list.*

*And the year is not even half over.*

*November 16:*

*Miss Diary, I am very excited! Tonight I am going to check out at least two frat parties. I am going to have some amazing things to tell you after tonight. I am on the prowl!*

KAPPA SIGMA FRATERNITY
November 16:

*I rolled over on this guy, not that I wanted to, but he was passed-the-fuck-out, and I needed to go back to the party, so I leaned over his massive hairy ape-like chest, struggling to get out of bed, but I must have aroused him into consciousness because he heaved and sighed like a beached walrus, uttering gross snorting noises that sounded like a stuffed pig belching, and when he actually spoke, muttering something stupid like, Do you have to go to the bathroom? I lied and said, Yes. So I rolled over him, inadvertently smelling his funky armpit as I swung my legs around and planted them on the floor. I glanced back at tonight's pathetic love connection feeling sick to my stomach. Maybe it was the fact that his hairy belly stuck out from beneath his T-shirt. I realized (too late) that he was way too fat for me. How did I wind up sleeping with such an out of shape wingnut? Maybe I was losing my touch. Just before sneaking out the door I glanced at a night table noticing an unopened pack of condoms lying under a lamp shaped like a bust of Mick Jagger with his grotesque tongue sticking out at me. I only have a vague memory of fucking this guy, but I swear he told me he put a condom on. I couldn't care less about the football game or the homecoming festivities, but I wanted to get to know some of the Theta guys. Everyone says they're the coolest fraternity. I walked downstairs hoping nobody would notice that I came out of a fat dork's room. Someone was playing REM (or was it U2?) and a bunch of guys were dancing real spastic, bumping into each other, throwing themselves into a mosh pit with other sweaty, shirtless hormonal assholes. I couldn't dig it. Then drop-dead-gorgeous Everett Barnes came up to me and handed me a red Solo cup filled with grape juice and grain alcohol. I was hoping he would stick around, but all he did was give me his cup and said, I'll see you later.*

*In the next room, Kyle Barrow (who I slept with last year) was in the corner hitting on a skinny freshman clad in a Madonna T-shirt and painted-on red slacks. I heard that Kyle might have AIDS, but, so what (ha! ha!).*

*In the midst of a lot of confusion, some guy named Jubu asked me to smoke a joint of Colombian and I said, Okay, and we went up to his room which turned out to be right next to the room I just came from and Jubu said something about the guy in the next room being gay and I wondered if he meant the dude I just left. Whatever. Does he have a fat stomach? I asked, immediately feeling like a total loser for asking such a stupid question. Jubu looked at me kinda perplexed, drunk, swaying, (probably stoned already) and just mumbled incoherently. I sat down on a filthy green sofa littered with sticky candy, potato chips, pretzels and fast food wrappers. Surrounded by trash, the smell alone was enough to make an elephant pass out. I polished off the last of my drink feeling a little woozy. I guess it didn't have much grape juice in it. I heard Jubu scream from across the room, apparently pissed off because he couldn't find his bong. Bored and restless, palpable anger was seething within* me. Gazing around the room, I spotted the obligatory giant poster of Michael Jordan with his tongue hanging out, legs splayed while dunking a basketball. I would sleep with him, if I had the chance. Both of my legs were pumping nervously and suddenly my left shoe hit an object on the floor. I reached down and picked it up. It was an old baseball glove and I put it on my hand, although I wasn't sure if I had it on right. Wanna have a catch? I yelled to Jubu and looked across the room noticing his skinny ass sticking out of the closet still trying to find his stupid bong. I waited a few seconds and then hurled the baseball glove, hitting him squarely on the ass. What a great throw! I think he cried, Ouch! but I was too busy finding my way out the door.

In the hallway, some totally cheesy fat girl with green spiked hair wearing a Florida gator's T-shirt and fuck-me-red lipstick—who I saw fucking Carter Mason, III in the back of his BMW last week--- came up to me and said, Hello. And I said, Nice outfit. I peered into one of the rooms and spotted a loser freshman passed out on a leather sofa with her suckface mouth open like a dead fish on a boat dock. She didn't belong at all. Sarah Tobias came up to me and I asked her if she heard any gossip, especially about the freshmen whom we all hate. Sarah, who once fucked a guy and ate a sandwich at the same time, said one freshman gang-banged the whole lacrosse team.

Leaving Sarah, I staggered over to a window at the end of the hallway to get some fresh air. For a moment, staring up at the bleak, fathomless sky, I almost I felt good. My eyes drifted down to the parking lot below and I heard a rustling sound in the bushes near a big green dumpster. I spotted a couple of naked fratpeople fucking their brains out, trying their best to be quiet, but I heard murmurings like....fuck me...suck me...shit like that. I watched them for a couple minutes and nothing very interesting happened except when she got on top of him, lit a cigarette and blew smoke in his face. I thought that was classic.

I decided to leave this lame party and check out the Zete party next door. As I entered, A mob of drunken fraternity guys dressed in drab-green hospital gowns with stethoscopes dangling around their necks descended upon me screaming diseases in my ear and thrusting Solo plastic cups of Kool-Aid and grain alcohol in my face. The assaulting hoard felt like a swarm of locusts in my face, so I waved my hands in front of me, brushing them off as if they were annoying Paparazzi. Before I could escape entirely one of the "doctors" stuck a "I have herpes" badge on my halter top. Undaunted, I plunged through *the disease brigade, heading for the safety of another room. On the way, I was distracted by the sight of Wade Lowinsky hitting on a petite freshman wearing Guess jeans and a loose fitting pink blouse with the collar turned up.*

Moving forward, I was accosted by another student barging up to me carrying a red Solo cup and a bedpan loaded with a block of ice and purple juice.

"Hey, Red! Have a drink! It'll kill your herpes!"

"Thanks," I said, taking the cup from him. I took a quick sip, then glared at him. "Don't call me Red, okay?"

"What should I call you?"

"Lori."

"Well, I'm Jay. Nice to meet you. How's your drink?"

"It's fine. Look, I gotta go, okay?"

"Don't you want to get cured and make it upstairs?"

"Okay, I get it. You give everybody a disease and they have to drink some punch in order to get cured."

"Hey, it's not that simple! First of all, it's not just any punch, it has to be the punch designated for your disease, then after an exam, you get to go upstairs."

"Exam? From who?"

"Our team of doctors! You have to prove you drank enough to deserve the honor of life above this floor."

"Look, I don't even want to go upstairs, and this is the dumbest theme party I ever heard       of---"

Abruptly, a short, student wearing a Madras shirt rushed up to Jay, whispered something in his ear and then disappeared.

"Who was that?"

"Oh, that's Barry, our resident den mother. Poor guy worries about everything. He doesn't want everybody to get too fucked up."

I looked around the room. "Looks like he's too late, already."

"Yeah, it's hopeless."

"Whatever. See ya."

*I weaved my way past another throng of medical students trying not to spill my drink. I fought my way into an isolated hallway, locating a mirror beside a ripped poster of the Dallas Cowboy Cheerleaders. Standing in front of the mirror, I set down my drink, straightened out my top, carefully blotting my lips with a tissue from my purse, fluffed out the sides of my hair, and smoothed out my eyebrows with my index finger. I took the badge off and tossed it in a trashcan. Turning away from the mirror, I glanced back to see if I missed a flaw. I hadn't. I grabbed my drink, took a huge gulp, and finished it off. Then, I headed back to the kitchen area to grab a beer. As I approached the kitchen door, someone rushed up behind me, and grabbed my left boob. I quickly jerked the hand away, whirling around, to see a fratguy with a buzz cut, blue eyes, shiny white teeth, and a "I have AIDS" button pinned to his hospital gown. I hurled my fist at his face, catching him flush in the mouth.*

*"Ouch!" He screamed, checking his upper lip for traces of blood. "You got quite a punch!"*

*"Fuck you, asshole!"*

*"Oh, a feisty redhead! I like those!"*

*Gee, this guy is really original. I wonder how many times I've been called a feisty redhead. "Fuck off, okay?"*

*Bolting down the hall, I awkwardly bumped into another group of medical students before latching on to a chair in a nearby room. The room was empty except for an emaciated homely girl dressed in layers of black clothing sitting alone on the other side. Jesus, an EMO person. She's a dead ringer for a Muslim woman without the burka. With a face like that, she should be wearing a burka, ha, ha.*

*Suddenly, a couple walked up to me holding hands. I recognized the girl as Mary Ann Cramer, a student whom I despised.*

*"Hi Lori," said Mary Ann. "How are you doing? I haven't seen you in ages."*

*"Oh hi Mary Ann! Hey, I'm doing great! Say, you haven't seen Drew Pennington have you? He asked me to meet him here."*

*"No, I haven't seen him. Maybe he's gone upstairs already."*

*"Oh, right. Maybe he has. Thanks."*

*"Lori, this is Norman Oliver."*

*"Hi Norman. Glad to meet you."*

*"Well, we'll see you later. Bye Lori!"*

*"Bye!"*

*Moments after Mary Ann and her boyfriend left, I felt dizzy and uncomfortable. Hoping to avoid running into someone else I hated, I got up and walked gingerly towards the rear exit, my legs wobbling like two rubber hoses. Staggering uneasily towards the back porch, I smelled a peculiar odor. Lurching forward, I grabbed the back door, stumbled awkwardly down the stairs, spun around, then collapsed on a brown couch in the corner...*

*Whoa...sinking fast into oblivion...slipping into the throes of night-time malaria stupefaction... What the fuck? My body petrified, inert on this couch...muted, barely audible voices whispering in hushed secret tones...A line from an old movie materializes...Is that cannon fire or the sound of my heart pounding? Or is it just the wind howling in the night, rustling through imaginary trees? Drifting down...Above me, ancient Chinese chimes are pinging a serene rhythmic tune, like a timeworn tinkling piano in the wee wee hours before dawn when even the whores are fast asleep. But, then the wind swells in velocity...the chimes not soothing anymore, but tiny invisible darts piercing my ears, triggering ice pick ricochets, painful inner vibrations. I roll over to one side, hoping for a respite from the agony of chiming barbs, nameless voices, and night-time sweats. Nothing but random sounds. An old Madonna song "Material Girl" blasting out a car driving by the house. Aluminum beer cans rattling noisily down the street, followed by hysterical shouts from fraternity assholes. High-pitched squeals of laughter from a cluster of sorority girls. A growling, heavy vehicle rumbling down a gravel alleyway... the clanking of a loose window shutter against the side of a clapboard house. Somewhere...a lonely bohemian beats a bongo in his retro hophead pad... beat...beat...beat... down the bumpy stairs. My feet are so far away I can barely see them through the murkiness, sticking straight-up like two lonely ears of corn in Kansas. Something is very wrong. Someone, something hungry and primitive is leaning over me, prying my legs apart, coarse callused hands pawing, groping me everywhere. Is there more than one? Unfastening my bra strap...roughly rubbing my breasts with his greasy filthy hands. My heavy-lidded, doped-up eyes unable to open....hands are useless as boiled noodles. Sinking...sliding into the abyss...going, going in and out... sucking on my left tit, kissing me harshly on the lips with way too much force, slipping deep, deeper, forewarning, fiendish werewolves baying at the moon, or maybe it's another monster on top of me, ripping off my dress, loosening my silver leather belt, jerking it away from my waist with his repulsive strength, his greasy mechanic's forearm pressing down on my neck, pinning me to the couch, I am so helpless as the beast or another creature removes my black lace panties, grabbing my crotch, rubbing his hands around and around. Where* is everyone? *The bastard is overwhelming me, and I can't really do anything about this…him sucking on my right boob, while he feels me up all over, starts finger-fuckin' harder and harder, rubbing his face against my tits, then he finds my asshole and rubs it in a circular motion. I try to open my eyes but everything is just a blur. I'm barely breathing, and a stinking, hairy chest crashes on top of me, smothering me Gaaaa…gging chok…ing….Ah! Strangler mother of night! My body is powerless to stop this fiend from violating me, ripping me apart—large, bulging—painful thrusting, thrusting, pumping, plunging—stabbing, stabbing—driving, driving inside me—brutal, pitiless sorrow--- hands covering my mouth—Help! Stop! Please stop! But, he grips my mouth—shut tight. I bite the bastard's hand, then he slaps me across the face screaming, "Bitch!" I try to scream again, but the black-hearted hand seals my mouth, tiny, moist droplets of breath escaping my lips, barely keeping me alive.*

*Again, the sweat-soaked blackness…*

The stranger lurked outside the dormitory room window watching the entire repugnant scene unfold before his eyes, listening to sounds of drunken rough sex. He watched as the frat boy lay on top of her, driving his penis into her until he ejaculated, then immediately rolling over, and grabbing his clothes before slinking out the door. He lifted the window, crept into the room, and leaned over her exposed, passed-out body, only partially covered by a plain white sheet. Her emerald dress was a wrinkled mess above her head, turned inside out. He pulled it down over her and then gathered up her panties and bra and stuffed them in his coat pocket along with her purse. He carefully placed her legs together looping the silver belt around her waist and tightening the dress. Then he carefully lifted her into his arms like a lifeguard holding a drowning victim and placed her gently on the ground outside the window. He looked around to see if anyone had seen him. Seeing no one, he carried her away, disappearing into the darkness of the night.

*John David Wells*

## ONE WEEK LATER

*I will lie here very quiet and composed like that crazy dude at the end of* Psycho. *Then everyone will know I wouldn't harm a fly. And when I am rescued from this hospital dungeon I will be the new darling of the media, bombarded by movie scripts, Hollywood agents, commercial endorsements, and, of course, the* paparazzi. *I am not as stupid as that doctor thinks I am. He doesn't know this is really a good career move for me. He thinks I'm vegetating here, zoned-out on all those hallucinogens he's jamming down my throat, shooting in my veins.*

*Lifting my fingers to my cheek, I feel a disgusting scab has materialized in a foolish attempt to tarnish my beautiful complexion. I pick the crusty thing off my face and flick it away gently as if it was a lovely butterfly.*

*There must be something to do besides sit here chained to a chair waiting for those nasty nurses to come around. My Uncle Charles came by yesterday. He told me that we are going on a long ocean voyage to retrace the path of Ulysses. That should be fun. I wonder where my breasts are. I am covered in a dirty hospital gown that is way too big for me.*

*It's embarrassing. Honest to God, I cannot find my tits. Looking down, I can see my toes, but there isn't anything where my luscious breasts used to be. What was the point of that expensive boob-job? I make a mental note to ask a nurse about this new discovery. The nurses here really suck.*

*My father should never have forced me into acting when I was five years old. All those stupid children's plays like The Frog Princess and Jack in the Beanstalk. I must have been in a hundred dreadful plays for little children, the whole time being fondled by creepy directors begging for blow jobs from innocent young girls like me.*

*In the beginning, I didn't know what was going on. I thought it was strange that someone wanted to see me with no clothes on. I knew it was not right, but I was strangely attracted to the thought of someone wanting to see me naked and touch me in different places. I guess it was the attention. It's amazing how sick men are. In my short, glamorous career I have slept with the Velveteen Rabbit, Captain Hook, Dopey from* Snow White, *the Cheshire cat, Mickey Mouse, Goofy and the Tin Man. Somebody told me that a director made Judy Garland sing "Somewhere over the Rainbow" while giving him a*

90

*blow job. Now that's class! I figured if it was good enough for Judy Garland, it was good enough for me.*

*I saw that hairy creature the other night. We played a few hands of Pinochle, but one of his arms fell off right in the middle of the game and, well, it was really embarrassing. I asked him why he looked like a leprous wolverine and he told me he had a rough childhood in South Chicago. And I said, 'No shit. Living in that hellhole would turn anybody into a hideous monster.'*

*Today, I will just lie here real quiet and peaceful. I won't give anybody any trouble. The loony doctor thinks he can drive me crazy with drugs. Just because he's nuts, he thinks he can turn me into a burned-out acid mental case. When this movie is over the whole world will know that I am a really nice person. After all, I wouldn't harm a fly...*

"How was that, Mr. Hitchcock? Was it a good take?"

Someone clapped their hands methodically three times.

"Is that you Mr. Hitchcock?"

"No, sweetheart, it's me. That was a wonderful monologue, but it's hardly a stretch for you to play an insane murderess."

The captive woman peered into the darkness, spotting a pair of shadowy khaki pants and brown shoes below the bottom half of the dimly-lit circle surrounding her.

"What are you talking about? Get me out of here!"

"And where do you think you are?"

"At the studio—no, I'm stuck in this hospital dungeon. It's your fault!"

"You don't know where you are, do you? Trust me, you are not in a movie studio. And you think you might be in a hospital? Why? Because you are sitting in a chair wearing a green hospital gown? Well, at least I know the drugs are working."

"What are you saying? I'm confused. Where's Mr. Hitchcock? Let me out of here! I am dying!"

"You cannot leave and transmit the plague."

"What plague? Are you crazy?"

"Yes."

"But, I don't have a plague!"

"Yes, you do. If you get loose, the whole world will be annihilated."

"How could I do that? I'm just a poor college student!"

"What was all that talk in your diary about giving AIDS to guys on purpose?"

"What? Did you read my diary?"

"Yes, it was quite informative."

"That wasn't true! I made up all that disgusting stuff!"

"Why?"

"I don't know! I was just fantasizing!"

"You have quite an imagination,"

"Yes! I was just imaging all that bad stuff happening."

"Well, in that case, I imagine that you should be punished."

"Goodbye, my dear."

The man turned, disappearing beyond the edge of the circle.

"Wait! You're not going to hurt me are you?"

A thin smile spread across his face; a monotone voice fading in the darkness, "No, of course not. I wouldn't harm a fly."

*TWO WEEKS LATER*

Detective Winslow approached the house, unsnapped the shoulder holster of his Glock 17, withdrew the weapon, holding it firmly behind his back. With his other hand, he padded his hip to make sure his backup Smith and Wesson snub-nosed .38 was secure. Winslow walked up the steps and knocked on the door. He waited a few moments, then rapped on the door again. Finally, he heard the man's tired voice at the door. "Who is it?"

This is detective Winslow, Chicago Police Department. I need to talk to you."

"About what?"

"A missing person."

"Can't it wait until tomorrow?"

"Sorry, we're working twenty-four/seven on this case and I need to ask you a couple questions."

The man hesitated, then cracked the door open. Winslow glimpsed a sliver of light, then savagely rammed the door open with his shoulder, cupping the Glock with both hands. The man spiraled across the room, landing awkwardly on a trashcan in the corner, spilling debris all over him. The man screaming, "Jesus Christ! What the fuck?"

"I'll tell you what the fuck! Now get up!"

The man shook off bits of trash, bracing himself against the living room wall. Winslow went into the kitchen, grabbed a chair and placed it in the middle of the room. "Sit your ass down here!"

"What are you doing?"

The man stutter-stepped to the chair like a dead-man-walking to the gas chamber. Winslow held the gun on him as he ransacked the kitchen drawers for a piece of rope. He found a frayed section of clothesline, came back into the living room and tied the man's arms around his back. He went back into the kitchen and got another chair, placing it directly in front of the man.

"Okay. We're gonna have a little talk."

"I have nothing to say."

"I'm afraid you do. Now, tell me what you did with Lori Ballantine. Is she in the cellar?"

"This is crazy! I have no idea! What are you doing? I want a lawyer!"

"Really? Do you have a phone?"

"No, I just moved---"

"No, problem. I'll go get my cell out of the car. You want a lawyer, right?"

"Of course."

"Well, then I'll have to arrest you and take you downtown. Do you know what that means?

"No."

"You'll be out of my hands. I won't be able to help you. If fact, I'll do everything I can to make sure you fry in the electric chair."

"For what?"

"For murdering Lori Ballantine. Now, you listen to me. If you let me help you—if you cooperate with me—just me—I'll fight every goddamn prosecutor in this city to send you to a mental hospital instead of death row. You are sick. Don't you see you need help? You want to die a horrible death before you have a chance to regain your sanity?"

The man remained speechless. Winslow reached into his coat pocket and produced a flask of Jack Daniels whiskey. He unscrewed the cap and slugged down a mouthful. "You want a swig?"

"Sure." The man reached over, took the flash and belted down a shot. His body shuddered, his head shaking vigorously from side-to-side. "Whew! That shit's powerful!"

"Unlike most things," said Winslow. "It works every time."

"Must be nice. I don't know anything that works every time."

Winslow nodded. "Most people don't know how they are going to feel from one minute to the next, but with this flask…every time I take a sip, I know exactly how I am going to feel in a matter of seconds."

"Can't you do that without booze?"

"No."

The two men sat facing each other, silent for a few moments.

Finally, the man asked, "Are you saying I am insane?"

"Yes."

The man closed his eyes, his head slumping into his chest. Winslow waited. When the man lifted his head again, he was crying.

"It's not my fault…honestly, I never meant to harm anyone, but that bastard Satan kept demanding it was my solemn duty—like I was his obedient foot soldier!

He's the one who should be going to the electric chair!"

"Where is she?"

Byron's mind wandered to a distant, remote interior place…

*"I knew it my heart it was wrong. But, the devil was so convincing. It was like he was my lord…my savior…and he deceived me…took my mind… and for what? I am sick of hearing him…sick to death of his insidious horrible schemes, showing me nothing but hatred, vengeance and demise. I should never have listened to him."*

"Tell me where she is."

Byron lifted his head, heavy vapor clouding his drooping eyes. "Okay, detective, I will tell you. But please, I am very thirsty. Can I have a glass of ice water?"

Winslow stood up from the chair keeping the gun pointed at the man. He went into the kitchen, grabbed a glass from the cabinet and poured water from the sink. Holding the glass in one hand and his revolver in the other, he walked back into the living room.

"Okay, here you are."

"I said ice water."

Winslow shrugged. He turned and strode to the refrigerator and opened the freezer door. As if slammed in the gut by a loaded cannonball, Winslow fell backwards on the kitchen counter, the glass in his hand flying, shattering to pieces on the floor. He clumsily swung the gun around in the man's direction. He was still motionless; a stupid grin pasted on his vacant face. His shirt drenched with water, Winslow crept up to the freezer door as if it might unleash all the evil forces into the world. Once again, he slowly opened the door.

Lori Ballantine was staring at him through frozen ice-blue eyes.

# Boots of Spanish Leather

I first met Anastasia in a Moscow bar after sneaking out of the Bolshoi Theater during the second act of the ballet *La Bayadere.* I was invited on a Moscow trip by a colleague who needed my help chaperoning a group of students as part of a short January course abroad. The students' appreciation of the fine arts far exceeded mine and after an hour the desire for a cold beer surpassed my interest in high culture. I ducked out of the theater and walked across the street to Katie O'Shea's Irish bar and restaurant. As I entered, I was greeted with a broad smile by a pretty young lady with long blond hair braided in pigtails. In spite of the cold, she was wearing a short emerald shirt, long brown stockings, and a light green soccer jersey.

"Can I help you?" she asked in English.

"How did you know I spoke English? Is it that obvious I am a foreigner?"

The girl laughed. "Oh, I can tell?"

"I'll just take a seat at the bar."

"Very well."

I strode across the room towards a classy antique mahogany bar. A few people were dining at white silk covered tables lining the perimeter of the room. I noticed an attractive woman sitting alone at the bar, and chose a stool next her. From the other end of the bar a brutish-looking bartender with a shaved head approached me sporting a sleeveless Black Sabbath T-shirt. Both arms were riddled with tattoos illustrating grotesque red devils, hairy monsters, and bloodthirsty werewolves.

"What can I get for you?"

"Just a Stella Artois draft."

"Coming right up."

Staring straight ahead, I suddenly felt uneasy, sensing the presence of Anastasia. A Frank Sinatra song was playing in the background. I tried to relax, but as I slightly turned my head, I heard the tiny bones in my neck creaking. I felt droplets of cold sweat trickling down my forehead. Finally, I glanced at her, wiping my forehead with my sleeve, and swallowing so hard, I was afraid she could hear the muscles in my throat constricting.

"Do you speak English?" I asked.

"Yes," she replied. "Are you American?"

"Yes. I just walked out of the ballet."

The bartender came back and placed the beer in front of me.

"To get a beer?" she asked, staring straight ahead.

"Should I feel guilty?"

"Not at all. Ballet is boring."

"So what do you do?"

"I'm a fashion photographer here on assignment."

"That's interesting."

She tilted her head, facing me. "No, it isn't," she declared, flashing a pair of glittering lavender-gray eyes. "Fashion is more boring than ballet. And you?"

"I'm here as a chaperon for some college kids."

"Aren't they a little old to have a chaperon?"

"That's what I said...I'm helping a friend."

"So I guess you're in Moscow on a class trip, giving your students a taste of culture."

"Right—except I just ran out on them. What are you drinking?"

"Scotch and soda."

"Can I buy you one?"

She ignored me and then glanced over my shoulder, quizzically looking up at the ceiling as if searching for the source of the music. "You like Sinatra?"

"Of course."

"He's the greatest singer of the twentieth century."

"I wouldn't argue with that."

"What's your name?"

"Tony Antonelli."

"So, you're Antony Antonelli."

"Something like that. My parents wanted to make sure I would always be recognized as Italian. What's yours?"

"Anastasia. You can buy me a drink, but not here. I know a jazz club."

"Near here?"

"We can take a taxi."

The taxi driver drove us to the middle of a darkened side street off Red Square and stopped in front of a blue neon sign flashing LENNY'S LOUNGE with an arrow pointing towards the sky. We entered a cramped foyer containing only an elevator and a printed sign: LENNY'S 8th FLOOR. As the door opened on the eighth floor, I followed Anastasia into an elegant, dimly-lit nightclub highlighted by a huge bay window overlooking the skyline of Moscow. The club had borrowed heavily from Parisian decor, adorning the place in muted colors of bronze, black and red. Mirrored *avant-garde* street mosaics and black and white photos of jazz greats lined the walls. To the left, inside a cozy alcove, a few elegantly dressed patrons lounged on cushy patterned sofas, chattering to each other, smoking cigarettes and sipping cocktails. Two narrow silver-topped bars with gold embossed leather chairs ran parallel to each other, spanning the length of the first room we entered. Anastasia led the way into a larger room occupied by a sultry black female in an emerald sequined cocktail dress playing the piano on a slowly rotating red platform. I heard her full-throated mellow voice floating from the speakers in a hushed whisper:

*The way your smile just beams,*
*The way you sing off key,*
*The way you haunt my dreams…*
*No no, they can't take that away from me.*

We walked past past a red and black checkered dance floor until Anastasia stopped at a table near the bay window displaying the colorful domes of Saint Basil's Cathedral.

"How do you like it?" asked Anastasia as we sat down.

"It's fantastic. Reminds me of a club I used to go to in New York."

"Even Moscow is getting some class these days."

"You mean Putin hasn't outlawed American jazz yet?"

Anastasia flashed a thin smile. "Just American democracy."

A skinny young man appeared before us wearing a white shirt, black vest and a bow-tie.

"Good evening," he said in English. "Something to drink?"

"Two whiskey and sodas," I said.

"Will that be all?"

"Yes."

I watched the waiter trailing away. "Does everybody speak English in Moscow?"

"If they want to get a job."

I nodded. "Americans are arrogant about the English language. They don't feel a need to learn any other."

"They should. You never know who you are talking to."

"What do you mean?"

"It's an old story. If you want to talk to your enemy, you speak German. If you want to talk to your lover, you speak French. If you want to talk to a friend, you speak Ukrainian."

"And English?"

"When you want to talk to everybody."

"That makes sense in a weird way," I said, flashing a bemused smile, and glancing at the city below us. "I never knew Moscow was so beautiful at night."

"Yes, the beauty of the night shines above the evil and corruption."

"We have corruption too. Look at Watergate."

"You have corruption within normal parameters—and you got rid of Nixon. In Russia he would never have been caught or thrown out of office."

"How about voting someone out of office?"

"Oh, you can vote alright. You can go to the polls and make your choice."

"And?"

"And you know how many choices you have?"

Before I could answer, she held up one forefinger. Then the waiter returned with our drinks. I held up my glass up, motioning to Anastasia, "To Russian-American relationships! The Cold War is over!"

Anastasia raised her glass, a broad smile warming her face. "I'll drink to that, Yankee!---But I have to tell you something. I'm not from Moscow. I'm from a small city in the Ukraine. I'm only here for a photo shoot."

"Well, then, let's drink to Russia getting the hell out of eastern Ukraine!"

Anastasia laughed and we clicked glasses, a gentle play of light glinting off her glass highlighting the rich tones of her natural blonde hair. We sat facing each other in front of the stage drinking whiskey and sodas, and listening to jazz standards by Billie Holiday and Ella Fitzgerald. I felt like I was in a Bogart movie in Paris during the 1940's, magically placed in a fashionable cinematic world where everyone was stylish, sophisticated, and dressed to the nines. The posh, intimate club seemed to expand outwardly while undergoing an atmospheric transformation, filling up fast with high class clientele. I spotted lovely ladies dolled up in diamond-studded silky evening dresses sipping crystal flutes of champagne and smoking long cigarettes set in sterling silver holders. They sashayed around the dance floor, flashing easy smiles while flirting with suave young men in tailored black tuxedos. On a spiral stairway, a handsome man with matinee-idol good looks cupped a snifter of golden whiskey, and then placed a soft kiss on a striking brunette clad in a long slinky red dress. A pair of young lovers passed by, drifting off for a secret meeting, disappearing into the shadows between the walls. And I was in the middle of it all—a dashing leading man falling under the bewitching spell of an awesomely beautiful, mysterious, intelligent, and charming lady. If there was love on earth, this had to be it.

As the surrealistic evening wore on, Anastasia melded into my fantasy. She was easily the most exquisite, charming lady in the club, and all the denizens of the night stared with wild wonder at the fine-looking American gentleman slow dancing with his Russian beauty as the jazz singer sang a lovely, plaintive "Smoke Gets in Your Eyes."

I knew I had to see her again. We exchanged contact information, and promised to stay in touch. I remember late in the evening asking her if I could visit her in her hometown of Nikolaev. She replied, "I'd love for you to come."

As soon as I returned to the to the United States I Skyped Anastasia right away, hoping to make plans for visiting her hometown. When she came on the screen she had just returned from yoga class, looking fabulous in a bright blue jogging outfit.

"How are things going? I asked.

"Oh fine. I just came back from my yoga class. It makes me feel so alive and relaxed."

"I would like to practice yoga myself. There are some great instructional videos on YouTube."

"You should do that! It's good for you!" she exclaimed.

"Listen, remember when we talked about me visiting you in Nikolaev."

"Oh yes, I remember."

"Well, how is your schedule in...let's say, the middle of March?"

"Oh, I don't know."

"What?"

"Well, that will be a busy time for me...I'm taking classes at the university and I have a lot of tests, and things."

"What are you studying?"

"Hotel management."

"Oh...well...I don't want to interfere with your studies. They are more important than me, that's for sure. When are courses over for good?"

"May."

"I might be able to make the trip in May. Do you think you can spend some time with me in May?"

"Do you know how long you can stay?"

"Two—maybe three weeks."

"I can be free for a weekend. We could go out to dinner."

"Dinner?"

"Is that all right?"

"Sure. It's not every woman who has a man traveling 3,000 miles just to have dinner with them. You must have some crazy magnetic power over men!"

"Oh, that's silly. You're not coming here just for me, are you?"

"Well...yeah."

"But, I told you I don't have much time..."

"I understand. I'm not going to interfere with your studies."

"Are you sure there are no other girls?"

"Other girls? No."

"Maybe you should contact some of them...in case I am very busy."

"You mean on a dating, marriage site?"

"Yes, there are thousands of Ukrainian girls who would love to meet a nice man from America."

"I know, but..."

"I'm sorry, Tony, but I must go. I'm tired."

"I understand. Do you want me to bring you a gift?"

"A gift?"

"Yes, something to remember me by."

"I don't know. What do you have in mind?"

"Something material. Maybe boots of Spanish leather."

# Savage Glitteration in the Night

Independent horror film producer Jonathon Wainwright owned an entire block in the city of Baltimore. The vast studio complex was originally an industrial building used to manufacture heavy duty machine tools and constructed with truckloads of identical red bricks which over the years chipped and faded into lackluster shades of orange, and gray. The creatively-challenged designers built such a dull and featureless structure as to virtually guarantee it would someday be an abandoned relic of the past, a permanent ugly splotch in the neighborhood. The only evidence outside the building that it was not deserted was a two-foot square bronze sign WAINWRIGHT PRODUCTIONS, INC. bolted to the side of the main door.

Each of the four floors contained a row of thirteen weathered wooden windows, all of them exactly the same size and covered by dark, sooty shades pulled down tight to prevent anyone from seeing inside the building. On nights when Wainwright hosted a party the shades were still closed, but passersby could glimpse flickering lights within illuminating shadowy figures waving their hands, shaking their booties, hoisting drinks, falling down and throwing up. On the roof a series of multi-colored spotlights aimed at the sky spun around in circles, crisscrossing each other.

Residents were intrigued by the sight of the neighborhood eyesore suddenly transformed into a riotous party of Mardi Gras proportions. Bass drums the size of hot tubs and amped-up electric guitars blasted away from inside, giving the illusion that the building was swaying back and forth to a disco beat. It was a cold night, but a few hardy souls huddled together on the stoops curiously gazing across the street. Tonight there seemed to be something special happening as more and more cars drove into the entrance, met by young male valet parking attendants clad in black pants, white shirts, and thick burgundy waistcoats.

Lamont Richards came out of a row house, joining his Aunt Grace who was sitting on the stoop nursing a 40-ounce Pabst Blue Ribbon. "What's going on over there?" he asked.

"Seems like a pretty big party," said Grace, nodding in the direction of the building.

Peering across the street, Lamont saw three luxury cars lined up in front of the entrance. A group of older, well-dressed couples emerged from their cars, handing keys to a valet. "Damn," said Lamont. "Look at that rich bitch over there."

Grace spotted an elderly woman being helped out of a shiny black Bentley driven by a dapper gentleman in a tuxedo accentuated by a white silk scarf draped rakishly around his neck. As the valet drove away, Grace got a good look at the woman. She was elegantly dressed in a peach-colored strapless evening gown with silver trim, and flashing an array of diamonds shimmering in the night like a tiny constellation of stars. Grace took a sip of PBR, her mouth sagging into a frown. "Dag, what are those people doing here? This ain't Park Avenue."

Lamont jutted his chin towards the warehouse. "There's something going on Grace. We're just not part of it."

After arriving, the guests were led to an antique oak door where one of the doormen formally opened it for them. By nine o'clock the parking lot was almost full. Lamont, Grace and a few die-hard neighbors continued hanging out on the chilly stoops watching silhouettes shimmering across the windows like dancing shadows.

Two blocks away, Donny and Constance Manchester sat on a bench in an isolated bus stop shelter shivering from the cold. Constance pulled a wad of crumpled tinfoil from her purse, carefully unwrapped it, revealing a small mound of white powder. Donny sat with his knee caps pumping, glancing furtively up and down the dark barren street. "What's that? Coke?"

"No my love," said Constance. "It's crystal meth—the best. I already did two lines. I got it from some stoner chick named Lisbeth."

"Sounds good to me."

After dumping the meth on the bench, Constance took a nail file from her purse and surgically chopped the pile into six straight lines. Rolling up a five dollar bill, she quickly snorted three of them before handed the bill to Donny who snorted his lines. Then, Constance grabbed Donny by the arm and couple bolted rapidly from the bus stop, racing as fast as they could down the block towards the party, arriving huffing and puffing, grasping their knees with both hands, and trying to catch their breath while laughing hysterically in between jerky gasps for air. Two bored, stone-faced doormen at the entrance watched them for a few seconds. One of them strode over to the couple. "May I help you?"

"I'm Donny Manchester…the uh…whew! I'm the actor in the movie… Mr. Wainwright's movie! This is my wife Constance. We were invite---"

"Just a minute sir," interrupted the doorman. He slipped inside, but was back momentarily. "Please come in. Welcome to Mr. Wainwright's party. The hostess will be with you in a moment."

As the doorman held the door open, the couple entered an expansive ornate reception area. Constance stared pie-eyed at the impressive room, compulsively twisting her purse as if it was a wet dishrag. Donny's mouth gaped open and he clutched his stomach as if someone landed a punch, his face flushing a pallid shade of pink. He leaned on Constance for support, tiny white flecks rising from his burning eyes like ash from a fire. Shaking him by the shoulders, Constance cried, "Donny Are you all right?" grabbing him by the waist, and dragging him awkwardly past two hatcheck girls wearing identical emerald gowns and Lauren Bacall peek-a-boo hairstyles. Constance set her husband down on one of the plush velvet divans on the other side of the room. "It's okay, honey. Are you all right?" Donny leaned back, resting his head on the back of the divan. Constance hoisted him up like a baby in a highchair. "What happened Donny?"

"I don't know," he muttered. "This place is…overwhelming."

Constance looked up, surveying the reception area which was layered with French Savonnerie carpets patterned with densely massed flowers against marine blue backgrounds. The room was lavishly stocked with colorful antique divans carved in intricate designs, tapestry armchairs in gilded walnut, a genuine Steinway piano, and marble pedestals supporting busts of Greek philosophers, Two gilt wood mirrors flanked the sides of a French limestone fireplace. A collection of classical Renaissance paintings hung from the glossy burgundy walls, illuminated by golden tubular beams angling down from the ceiling.

Directly across from Constance, three blonde-haired young ladies decked out in matching Thierry Mugler black cocktail dresses sat together at a French tableau table with fancy stationary and fountain pens placed in front of them. The top of the table was decorated with three gold candelabras bathing the young ladies in soft candlelight. A silver crystal chandelier hovered over the middle of the room, glittering like a spaceship ready to land.

Donny opened his eyes, rubbing them into focus with both hands. An attractive older woman abruptly materialized in front of them clad in a Christian Lacroix magenta evening gown, offering a broad effusive smile while daintily lifting her arm and extending a hand to Donny. "Donny! Constance! Welcome to the party! My name is Zelda de Haven. I am the hostess for tonight's festivities. Mr. Wainwright has told us all about you! And Constance, so lovely to meet you! I've heard all about you—you're even more beautiful than I imagined!"

"Thank you," said Constance, politely shaking her hand.

"Do we have to check in, or anything?" asked Donny, letting go of her hand.

"Of course not, my dears. Come with me!" exclaimed Zelda, leading the couple through a giant mahogany door, exposing a sprawling arena the size of a football field exploding with bright lights, loud music, and a multitude of drunken revelers.

"Now, Donny and Constance" said Zelda, batting her fake eyelashes as she waved vigorously to random guests passing by. "I must tell Jonathon you are here! You are the last cast member to arrive! Have you seen Julie Masters"

"No," said Donny.

"Well, she's just about the most precious thing you've ever seen in your life. And what an actress! This film will make history! Well, I must be going...Oh, I should tell you. Jonathon never makes an entrance before eleven o'clock. He's such a *prima donna*! Well, tootles, my darlings!" cried Zelda before disappearing into a throng of people.

"Jesus," muttered Donny. "Was she for real?"

"Of course not, darling," responded Constance. "If her real name is Zelda de Haven, then I'm Greta Garbo. She said the word *tootles*, for Christ's sake."

The party lights and frenzied dancing seemed to unfold for miles. Constance was cranked up, wire, and totally spun, her eyes feasting on the galaxy of flashing lights and thunderous music, Donna Summer's "Hot Stuff" pulsating from nearby speakers. A few yards away, a skinny black DJ sporting a black fedora and sunglasses stood behind a glass partition flipping stacks of albums and rapping to an uproarious mob dancing on a laser-lighted floor while an electrified mirror ball spun dizzily from the ceiling. Constance eyed Donny standing stiffly and forlorn as if he was waiting in line at the welfare office. Even wired on speed Donny was not a social butterfly.

"Well, Mr. Manchester," asked Constance, "What do you think about your boss' party?"

Donny smiled, shrugging. "Gee, couldn't the guy at least put out some crackers and cheese?"

"I think Mr. Wainwright probably owns a cracker *and* a cheese company."

Emerging from the crowd, a man in his late thirties sidled up to the couple, offering his hand to Donny. Unshaven, well-toned and tanned, he wore a silver-sequined suit, matching shoes and a solid gray shirt. Constance thinking he looked like Don Johnson dressed like the Tin Man.

"Hey! Welcome to the party!" he exclaimed. "I'm James Cresson. You're Donny Manchester, right?"

Donny shook his hand. "Yes, how did you know?"

"I'm Jonathon's personal secretary. I saw your screen test—Magnificent! Then he glanced at Constance. "And who might you be?"

"I'm his wife Constance."

"Pleased to meet you! I was going to ask you to dance, but I never move in on another man's wife--- at least not in front of him!"

Donny laughed. "I know Constance has been dying to hit the dance floor. Go on, have some fun."

"Are you sure it's okay?" asked Constance.

"Sure, no problem. They've got fifty bars here. I'll be at one of them, don't worry."

"Okay," said Constance. "But don't get lost. I'll see you at the bar!"

James and Constance rushed off, but before they were out of sight he heard James yelling in Constance's ear, "Did you know David Lee Roth is here?"

Donny wandered away from the dance floor passing a long table with a white silk tablecloth containing enough food and drinks to host the summer Olympics. A bevy of good-looking clean-cut waiters and waitresses wearing matching black and red outfits scuttled around the table serving guests and resupplying stock from the kitchen in the back. Donny continued strolling leisurely down the wide carpeted aisle passing a glitzy nightclub, a Prince song blaring amid a blitzkrieg of vivid laser lights. Inside the club, he noticed a rectangular marble-topped bar encircled by narrow tubes of bedazzling red neon lights. Four giant golden metal cages were placed on top of each corner with a stripper pole running down the middle. Two of the cages were occupied by a pair of sexy female dancers costumed in pink thongs and nickel-sized pasties. In the other cages, two Chippendale hotties shook their booties clothed in nothing but lime green florescent jock straps.

Donny kept moving until he arrived at a shiny circular chrome bar tinted with an ocean blue top, the name "Rick's" scrolled in cursive blue letters above the mirror behind the bar. He took a seat on a stool shaped like a big plastic salad bowl impaled on a chrome stick. Sinking down low, he leaned forward, propping his elbows up on the counter. A handsome, older bartender with a Clark Gable mustache wearing a black vest, white shirt and black bow-tie motioned to him as he was serving a Cindy Lauper impersonator. Donny took a second glance thinking, *Maybe it is Cindy Lauper.* He hated sitting low at a bar, feeling as if he should be ordering a jar of Gerber's baby food. After serving Cindy her drink, the bartender approached him smiling broadly, "Good evening! What can I get for you?"

"A gin and tonic will be fine. By the way, I'll bite. Why the name Rick's?"

The bartender nodded in the distance. "Well, the next bar is called Dempsey's and the one after that is Smokey Joe's---"

"Got it," interjected Donny. "All named after famous bars. I don't suppose Bogie is coming in tonight?"

The bartender chuckled. "No, but you can find Mr. Hemingway down at Smokey Joe's. He's been there all day."

Donny glanced at one of the speakers above the bar. "I like the music too. Is that Ella Fitzgerald?"

"Right," said the bartender. Nothing but forties jazz and blues here— the way Bogart would have liked it."

Donny nodded. "It's better than that disco shit."

"Hell, I don't call that real music. Gin and tonic, right? Coming right up!"

Donny swiveled around in his stool checking out a nightclub down from the bar playing loud tribal-techno music to young adults gyrating on the floor like epileptic monkeys. The bartender returned with his drink. "Here you are, buddy."

"Thanks. I'm Donny by the way."

The bartender reached out and shook his hand. "Nick. Pleased to meet you."

Nick noticed two women sidling up to the bar, and quickly left. One of the women clad in a pink leather mini-dress, teal tank-top and forest green leg warmers concealed her face behind a black mesh veil studded with tiny silver stars. Her companion with short spiked green hair wore a gold lame leather top with copper-colored pants, and pointy brown suede boots. They were immediately joined by a pimply kid no older than seventeen sprouting a gnarly nest of bleached-blond hair, wearing baggy jeans and a Punky Brewster T-shirt. Donny could feel himself aging by the minute. Taking a sip of his drink, he glanced in the mirror in front of him. As the minty taste cooled the back of his throat, he zoned-in on the reflection of the man frowning and holding a gin and tonic, wondering how that guy had gotten so old, so soon.

Swiveling around on his stool like a tiny tot, he spotted another bar to his left with a country and western theme complete with a naked girl riding a mechanic bull while waving a bottle of Wild Turkey in the air. In front of the bar, three shit-faced college girls with watermelon-size tits danced together, wildly whooping it up, jumping up and down, and then simultaneously rolling up their tops and tossing them over to the bartenders. The crowd went nuts. Donny swiveled another 90 degrees locating a darkened bar playing a song by The Cure. In a shadowy corner two heroin glum punks shrouded in black hoodies stood up slowly and shambled towards the bathroom for a quick blast. They passed by an elderly gentleman in a purple John Travolta jumpsuit wearing Armani wraparound sunglasses sitting in a French chaise lounge surrounded by three nubile nymphets drinking champagne, a rolled-up thousand dollar bill sticking out his left nostril. Donny turned back around facing Nick who was a few feet away bending down, sneaking a shot of Jameson's whiskey. Donny polished off his drink in one gulp, staring into the glass as if answers to his problems were written on the bottom. He was out of his element and he knew it. He was not totally comfortable with hyped-up-super-revved-up glitteration in the night, the stark, double-dyed illumination of the dark, seedy and gloomy underbelly of the city's shadowy netherworld. Raising his empty glass towards Nick, it occurred to him that the bartender might be the most normal person in the building. "Say Nick, do you know Mr. Wainwright by any chance?"

"Not really," said Nick, reaching for a cocktail glass. "I see him occasionally going up the elevator."

"Elevator?"

"Over there."

Donny looked where Nick was pointing, noticing for the first time a glass enclosed elevator bracketed by two heavy steel girders. "So, he goes up there? What for?"

"You don't know?" asked Nick, eyeing him suspiciously.

"Should I?"

"Maybe not," said Nick, loading the glass with ice and pouring in a healthy shot of gin. "I guess this is your first time." Finishing off the drink with a splash of tonic and slice of lime, Nick set it down in front of Donny. "Well, it's no big secret. This isn't the only floor, you know. There are four altogether."

Donny took a sip of his drink, poking the lime up and down. "Four?"

"This floor is normally a giant film studio. Certain select guests are allowed on the second floor. The third floor is reserved for…*really* special guests…and nobody gets to the fourth floor."

"Sounds very mysterious."

"It's none of my business."

"So, what's on the second floor?"

"Different rooms—excuse me, I'll be back."

Donny gazed across the other side of the massive complex spotting a wrought iron spiral staircase and a plain white door posted with a NO ADMITTANCE sign. Amid the cacophony of omnipresent noise, lights and music, Nick heard a faint murmur in his head, a slight buzzing as if someone was holding an electric razor close his ear. He tried ignoring the sound and concentrated on the song playing, a haunting saxophone solo. Nick returned from serving a customer; Donny looked him, the buzzing getting louder. "You were telling me about the second floor—different rooms."

"Well," said Nick, This probably won't surprise you. This place is practically an extension of the Playboy Club. Mr. Wainwright has special rooms that cater to certain clientele."

"Like?"

Nick tilted his head and grabbed his chin as if trying to remember his own telephone number. "Well...there's the waterbed room, the mirror room, the massage room, the bondage room, the...accessories, toys room, and there's even a Marilyn Monroe room."

"What's that?" asked Donny, the buzzing now feeling like a lit fuse attached to his brain.

"All the women in the room look exactly like Marilyn Monroe—only you have to guess which ones are really female."

Nick inadvertently slapping the side of his head with his palm, "I'd hate to guess wrong."

"Believe me," said Nick. "It's harder than you think."

"There you are!" cried Constance, draping her arm around Donny's shoulder. "I thought I'd never find you!"

"Actually, I didn't get very far."

"I know. This place is *huge!* Have you seen Mr. Wainwright?"

"No, not yet."

"How about the cast—your leading lady?"

"I haven't met anybody except Nick, the bartender."

"I had no idea your Mr. Wainwright was so filthy rich."

"Yeah," said Donny. He's got a few bucks." The buzzing suddenly stopping completely. "What happened to Mr. What's-His-Name, the silver guy?"

"Oh, James, his personal secretary. Gay as the day is long, but a great dancer. Do you know there's an upstairs?"

"Yes, Nick's been telling me about it. It's sounds very…extravagant."

From out of nowhere two sturdy muscular men wearing blue-gray uniforms with STAFF etched into their shirts walked up to the couple. One of them stood in front of Donny. "Are you Donny Manchester?"

"Yes."

"Can you come with us, please."

"Really, what for?"

"Mr. Wainwright has a surprise for you."

"Okay, but can my wife come?"

"Sorry, not this time."

"All right," said Donny, a quizzical look on his face. "Honey, I'll be right back."

"No problem, dear," said Constance.

Donny and the two men disappeared into the crowd. Constance remained at the bar talking to Nick as more and more raucous party goers entered the warehouse.

A half-hour later, all the lights went out, and the music abruptly stopped leaving everyone in the warehouse suspended in total darkness. A few low-key murmurs drifted through the subdued crowd, but no one seemed particularly concerned. Without warning a lone spotlight struck the top floor of the glass-enclosed elevator, followed by a gradual descent to the floors below. When the creaking elevator reached the second floor the silent crowd could see the fuzzy outline of a man dressed in a black suit draped in a floor-length red cape holding something in his hand. As the elevator lurched to the ground floor, the doors slid open, and the occupant stepped out, lifting a microphone up to his mouth.

"Good evening, ladies and gentlemen!" shouted Jonathon Wainwright. "Are you having a good time!?"

"Yes!" a huge roar erupting from the stunned, expectant assemblage.

"Now, you all know why we are here tonight. This is a *super* special evening dedicated to the next great film by Wainwright Productions—*The Virus Girl!*"

More screaming, manic outbursts of applause.

"Look up in the sky! Is it a bird? A plane? No, it's the stars of the film!"

From high above the ceiling clear up to the rafters, two gigantic spotlights swirled around and around as if it was the opening of a Hollywood premiere. The spotlights intersected with each other until one of them landed on Julie Masters smiling thinly as she sat in a metal harness resembling an ornate lawn chair decorated like an Egyptian throne. The harness was suspended from one of catwalks by a series of pulleys and supported by means of a galvanized steel cable split into four smaller cables affixed to each side of the harness. Momentarily, another spotlight landed on Donny perched a hundred feet opposite his co-star sitting in a similar decorated harness. All eyes gazed skyward at Wainwright's latest dramatic spectacle.

"Now," continued Wainwright, "It's time to introduce our leading man and our leading lady! Let's give a big hearty Baltimore welcome to the newest members of the Wainwright dream team! Donny Manchester and Julie Masters!"

In the rafters, staff members unhooked the attached harnesses, simultaneously releasing Donny and Julie towards each other. Like two circus trapeze artists flying through the air on high-flying trapezes, the two actors flew across the top of the warehouse, swinging back and forth supported by two giant steel pendulums.

The joyous, excitable throng of party goers strained their necks to the rafters, gaping at the surprising circus act, eye-balling the roving spotlights illuminating the two actors, sailing past each other, nearly shaking hands. Laughing uproariously, they were centrifugally catapulted towards each other, swinging to and fro while slowly descending. On the fourth passing, Donny started to reach out his hand, but withdrew quickly as the harnesses came dangerously close to colliding. Donny noticed a look of concern on Julie's face as he passed her. As they swung back again, they were heading straight for each other, on a collision course, rapidly gaining speed. Donny yelling up at the rafters, "Hey, lookout!" praying the staff would alter the trajectory of the pendulums. But to his horror, Julie was swinging right at him full force. At the last second, he braced for impact before the harnesses brutally collided in mid-air high above the warehouse floor, the cables scissoring, and grotesquely entangling, causing the harnesses to tilt upward, dumping Julie out of her seat, and sending her pummeling to earth.

Donny struggled to grip the arm of the chair with one hand, and for a frightening grotesque moment dangled helplessly in the air, before letting go and dropping to the bottomless abyss below. Hurling crazily through the air, Donny looked down, searching for Constance, but all he saw was a mind-blowing explosion of effulgent luminescence, a kaleidoscopic neon dreamscape bursting through the savage glitteration in the night.

# A Perfect Game on a Perfect Day

Collin Belinsky decided to visit his sister Maureen at the mental hospital in Goochland, Virginia. The temperature was dropping steadily as dark gray undulating clouds scuttled across the sky chilling the warmth of the sun in his path. Driving a vintage 1957 fire-engine red Chevy convertible, he picked up Route 250 and headed east towards Richmond. The winding road was a gray ribbon of asphalt running through lush green countryside dotted with bales of hay rolled into huge balls, horses grazing on small farms, quaint historical towns, and heavily forested areas populated with cedar, oak, and pine trees. Along the way, he stopped for gas, a bag of ice, and a six-pack of Budweiser at Willard's Stop and Go convenience store. After loading up the cooler with beer and ice, he cracked open a can and shoved it into a Baltimore Ravens coolie cup. Two beers later, he arrived at the open wrought iron gates of the hospital, and parked the car in a gravel parking lot beside three identical brown cars with government license plates. He strolled leisurely up a well-worn cement walkway to the entrance of an expansive red brick complex. The main building was located in the center of identical rectangular boxes joined together by spoke-like corridors with opaque, glass-covered canopies. The faded yellow windows looked like they had never been open. A ten-foot chain-link fence topped with circular bales of barbed wire spiraled around the grounds, as if the architects were determined to make the complex resemble a prison.

He passed a few patients loitering on the grounds dressed in plain white cotton gowns, heads bent, slouching aimlessly, obviously with no place to go. In a faded brown wooden gazebo surrounded by Leland cypress trees, an elderly patient sat talking to himself. Entering the building, Collin spotted a group of patients lounging in a day-room. They were watching TV, playing Checkers, staring into space, and smoking cigarettes. Two TV sets at each end of the room blared loudly as if competing with each other. One of them was currently showing *The Newlywed Game.* The walls, curtains, ceiling, furniture, rugs—even the patients—all blended into one another as if everything was painted the same drab green color. He continued straight ahead, approaching a fat lady in a loose-fitting tan dress with jet black hair pulled back tight in a bun. She was sitting behind a gray metal desk with her head lowered, reading a magazine. She looked up.

"Can I help you?"

"Yes, I'm here to see Maureen Fairmont.."

"Please have a seat."

The fat lady reached over, picked up a phone, and punched a few buttons. "Is Dr. Swanson still here? Okay. All right. Please tell her someone wants to speak to her in the lobby."

Minutes later, In a woman dressed in a stiff, starched white lab coat carrying a clipboard entered the lobby from a door marked PRIVATE adjacent to the receptionist's desk. She immediately came up to Collin walking stiffly as her lab coat. Collin thought he looked like a research assistant in a low-budget horror movie.

"Yes, may I help you?"

"I'm Collin Belinsky----Maureen Fairmont's brother."

"Dr. Swanson. Pleased to meet you."

"I'm just here to take Donna out for a short time. It's all been cleared, hasn't it?"

"Yes, of course, Mr. Belinsky. There's no problem. Come with me, please."

Dr. Swanson led Jackie through a doorway and down a narrow, dimly-lit hallway until they arrived at her office. She opened the door, motioning him to enter, then closed the door and disappeared down the hallway.

Collin sat in a deep burgundy leather chair facing her desk. It contained a neat pile of papers, a computer, printer, Fax machine, and two small vases filled with artificial flowers. In back of the desk there was a push-pin cork board with photographs of what he assumed were her husband, three children, and a black Labrador Retriever. Her diplomas from several colleges and universities were hung in precise rows along the sides of the cork board.

Minutes later, Dr. Swanson returned with Maureen trailing behind her, taking small, shuffling steps and looking downcast. Maureen trudged into the office, lifted her eyes to see her brother, and instantly became more animated, her eyes brightening like a car's high-beams switched on.

"Collin!" yelled Maureen, "Are we going out?" Turning quickly towards Dr. Swanson. "We can go out, can't we?"

"Yes, for a little while."

"Collin, do you have any cigarettes?"

"Not on me. But we'll get some."

"Come on! Let's get out of here! This place sucks!"

"Please return in two hours," said Dr. Swanson, adjusting a picture on her desk that did not need adjusting.

The couple walked down the hallway, through the lobby, and out the front door. Collin led Maureen to the car and opened the door for her.

"Cool car, bro! Can we get cigarettes now?"

"Sure."

"You still smoke?"

"No, I quit. So how's the hospital?"

"It's creepy. They got me on Haldol, but I really need Navane. This one psychiatrist was giving me thirty milligrams a day. Then they cut it back to ten because I was having side effects."

"Like what?"

"I don't know… couldn't think right."

Collin pulled out of the hospital, heading towards Route 250. "There's a convenience store down the street. We can get you some cigarettes. Is there any place you want to go?"

"Palmyra. Let's go to Palmyra."

"Okay. No problem."

"Can we go by Palmyra Park too?"

"Sure."

Collin pulled into the convenience store, purchased a pack of Marlboro Lights, and then returned to the car. He got back behind the wheel, started the car, and drove towards Palmyra.

As they traveled along, Maureen smoked one cigarette after another, smiling and laughing to herself. One minute she seemed like the happiest person alive; then suddenly she would utter a dark, ominous phrase like "other people are are cellular transparency." Collin stopped at a red light.

"Sis, you think that hospital is helping you?"

"Helping me what?"

"You know—get better…"

Maureen suddenly erupting in laughter. "That place couldn't help Bob Dylan sing a folk song."

"What are you laughing at?" asked Collin.

"He just said something funny."

"Who?"

"Bob Dylan."

"You're talking to Bob Dylan?"

"Of course, silly. I have his phone number.."

"Really"

"But he doesn't want me to give it to you."

"That's okay."

"He's coming to visit me next week."

"Are you sure?"

"Of course. He loves me. Why else would he write a song about me?"

"What song is that?"

"Sad-Eyed Lady of the Lowlands."

"Is that who you are?"

"Of course, little bro. I've got hollow cheeks. Look at my eyes."

"What about them?"

"Eyes like smoke, right?"

"Eyes like… green, you mean?"

"Feel my arm."

"Why?"

"Go on, feel it."

"Okay." Collin reaching over and touching Maureen's arm.

"Feels like silk, right?"

"Not really. Feels like you could use a meal or two---"

Collin turned, gazing into Donna's eyes. She was staring right through him, giving no hint that he was in the car. Her unblinking faraway opaque eyes were fixed on his chest. Then she slowly lifted her head.

"Little Bro," she muttered. "You have been drinking too much."

"Yes, I have."

"I knew it."

"How?"

"Your aura—it's diminished."

"My aura?"

"The light surrounding your body—it's not glowing like it should."

"How can you tell?"

"Are you serious?"

"Yes."

"Well, everybody has an aura. Everybody gives off a certain amount of light—like energy. Yours is barely lit up."

It occurred to Collin what was so different about all the dead bodies he had seen. He never realized it before; their aura was gone. No doubt his sister was right; he had an aura problem.

"The halo," said Maureen.

"Halo?"

"That's where it came from. The golden light surrounding a person. Didn't you ever see those Renaissance paintings?"

"Of course. It makes sense. I'll work on improving my aura, okay"

"That's a good idea."

"It's also called nimbus."

"What?"

"The circle of light around peoples' heads in those old paintings."

"Right."

"I love optical effects. Did you know nimbus is produced by ice crystals in the sky?"

"I didn't know that."

"For a smart person, there sure is a lot you don't know."

Minutes later, Collin pulled into the park, stopping at the basketball courts. "How's this?" he asked.

"Let's go up to the Little League field."

"Okay."

Collin drove up the street and parked next to the field. It had not changed much in twenty years.

"I know where we are," said Maureen.

"Where are we?"

"This is where you played the game."

"Do you remember?"

"Of course, silly. It was the Fourth of July."

"Yes, it was."

"Tell me the story, Collin."

"Sis, you've heard that story a hundred times."

"I know! Tell it again, Collin! Tell me again! It was the Fourth of July!"

"I don't know..."

"Come on! It was the Fourth of July!"

"Sis, really..."

"Collin please! It was the Fourth of July! The sun was shining down... like on a lake of precious stones! Vera Lincoln was in the stands!"

"Okay, but this is the last time."

"Sure, Collin"

Maureen smiled, leaned back in the seat, and closed her eyes.

"You know, Collin, my life hasn't been so great either."

It occurred to Collin that he was part of a world that composed and decomposed itself in an endless process of rebirth and mortality. And sometimes, in the darkest moments, you can only think about and remember the passing away of it all, even though lingering pain and regret weighs upon you like the ghosts of dead ancestors.

. Once more he glanced over at her. She was still lying back in the seat and appeared to be asleep. He turned the ignition to leave, but Maureen shouted, "Jackie, wait! Remember—it was the Fourth of July!"

Then Collin told his sister the story of the greatest day in his life. She insisted that he not leave out a single detail. And so he began, as always, by describing the way the blazing sun shone on the Little League field as if it was shining down on a lake of precious stones and continued all the way to the end of the story when he hit a grand slam homer to win the game.

When he finished, Maureen was smiling. "You played a perfect game on a perfect day."

Collin scanned the ballpark, taking one last look at the right field fence where he hit the home run. Then he started the car and drove Donna back to the hospital. He escorted her to the lobby, and soon an attendant was taking her to her room.

Before she disappeared behind a door, Donna turned, uttering a hard whisper: "Collin, go find your element!"

# Oriental Corpse Flowers Ascending

Alexis Stewart sat alone in the college student union gazing at an enormous plate glass window spanning the entire side of the lounge area. The midday sun streamed through the transparent wall, casting luminous shafts of light on a small group of students hanging out between classes. Staring intently at the angles created by the glistening rays, Alexis was dazzled by the sun's creation of a real life French Impressionist painting. Her focus was suddenly broken by her roommate Jody Taylor bursting through a side door, rushing up to her as if pursued by a gang of thieves. springing in the air, and waving her arms frantically, screaming, "Alexis, guess what!?"

"What?"

"I got the part!"

"What part?"

Plopping down in the booth, Jody flailed her arms as if she was yelling for help at the window of a burning building. "Leslie Ann Mitchell—the psycho co-ed from hell!"

"Awesome!" cried Alexis, pretending to know who Leslie Ann Mitchell the psycho co-ed from hell was.

"Can you believe it? I beat out all those Hollywood bitches."

"Are you talking about the audition you did this summer?"

"Don't you remember? I told you all about it. I can't believe I got the female lead in

Carlton Weinberg's new movie. He *loved* my screen test!"

"Carlton Weinberg? That creepy movie director?"

"He's not creepy. His pictures make millions of dollars."

"Jesus, Jody. The guy is a Hollywood joke."

"Oh please, he's a cult giant. They host film festivals in his honor."

"Okay...okay," muttered Alexis. "Where are they filming this masterpiece?"

"On location in Boston."

"What's it called?"

*"Psycho Sorority Drug Ring."*

"What's *that* about?"

"Well," said Jody, glancing at the mirror behind Alexis. "I haven't read the whole script, but it's about these crazy college girls who deal drugs to their friends."

"Are you serious?"

"Come on, Alexis. Don't be jealous."

Alexis fought off the urge to roll her eyes and point out that it will be a low budget movie headed straight to video. "All right, Jody. Congratulations."

"You don't understand!" squealed Joy, slapping her palms on the booth. "It's a serious commentary on our society."

Alexis nodded noncommittally, refraining from inquiring about the burning social issues in the upcoming film *Psycho Sorority Drug Ring.*

"What are you drinking?" asked Jody.

"A Diet Coke. Sally Witherspoon is waitressing. She'll be over soon."

Jody audibly sighed, ogling the mirror once more focusing on the minutia of her physical appearance, carefully selecting a loose strand of her shoulder-length flaming red hair, and held it up in front of her face, inspecting it as if it was a rare jewel. Alexis wanted to stick a knife down her throat. Taking a sip of her drink Alexis tried channeling her childhood ability to make people disappear by squeezing her eyes shut tight. She paused, praying Jody would vanish from her sight. Then she opened her eyes; Jody was still there. Alexis thinking, *Dear God, Jody is still here. Thanks a lot.*

"Do you think I need a haircut to fix these split ends?" asked Jody, twisting a lock of hair around her index finger, raising her voice several octaves, emitting a high-pitched squeal that sounded to Alexis like wounded words shrilling through a throat with serrated edges. *The knife. The knife I shove down her throat should have serrated edges—definitely.*

"Well..."

"Well what?" asked Alexis, daydreaming about serrated edges.

"My split ends! Do you think I need a haircut?"

"I don't know..."

Alexis glanced over again at the plate glass window. Shiny streams of sunlight reflected on a group of fresh-faced students wearing identical brightly-colored outfits, eye-blinding combinations of hot pink, lime green and canary yellow. She thought the Monet-like students resembled a host of spring flowers blooming in a bucolic countryside. The pastoral images of springtime contrasting sharply with dark blue spears of light shimmering off the glassy pond located directly outside the union.

"Alexis?"

"Huh?"

Alexis turned towards Jody, her head lolling drunkenly as if her neck was made of Silly Putty. All of a sudden she had trouble breathing, forcing short sputtering gasps of air into her lungs. *Was Jody sucking all the air out of the room?*

"You were spacing out," said Jody.

"Where?"

"Christ, where do you think?"

A waitress suddenly appeared before them.

"Oh hi, Sally. How are you?" asked Alexis.

"I'm fine. Would you like something to drink?"

"Yes, I'll have a Coke."

"Anything else?"

"No, not right now," said Alexis.

Alexis watched Sally walk over to another booth, and the glanced at the window again. "Will you look at those dark spears penetrating the glass over there? They're coming from the lake."

Jody gave the wall a quick look, shrugged, and took a sip of her Diet Coke. Alexis turned again, catching a glimpse of rolling cumulus clouds obliterating the sun, casting an ominous gray blanket over the pond and student union. Slumping further down in her seat, Alexis expelled a barely audible groan. *Back to Dullsville. Fade to black and white.*

Jody remained silent, preoccupied with her nails. Alexis decided it was hopeless. She could tell Jody that Jesus himself was giving away free lines of cocaine on the pool table, and it wouldn't make any difference.

Jody's obsession with her personal appearance dominated every fiber of her existence. Once again, the giant window caught Alexis' attention. At the lake, she spotted a mother mallard duck with her nose pointed in the air waddling across the pond, eight scurrying baby ducklings trailing frantically behind her. The comical youngsters paddled desperately to keep up with their resolute military-like mother who never bothered to look back to see if the little ones were keeping pace.

"I think I need more lip liner," declared Jody. "What do you think?"

*"Really* Jody? You put more red on and you're gonna glow in the dark."

"Very funny."

Twitching nervously on the brink of a panic attack, Alexis blurted out the first thing that popped to her mind. "Jody! I saw Susie Banford sitting on our basement floor stuffing a Little Debbie's cream pie in her face. It looked like a giant zit exploding from her mouth."

"Hey," said Jody, casting her eyes across the union. "Check out the hottie in the tan Dockers and blonde hair over by the pool table."

"Did you hear what I said?" Alexis wondering how Jody developed this modern talent for getting on her nerves.

"Sure, I heard you. What does she do with the vomit?"

"What?"

"What does a bulimic do with the vomit?"

"Gross, Jody, how would I know? What do you want to do? Start an investigation or something?"

"I was just wondering, that's all. You don't have to be so rude, you know."

Alexis became aware of a tingling sensation in her toes, like the prickly needle stings when they are thawing out from the bitter cold. Unexpectedly, the tiny needle barbs started gaining speed, moving rapidly up her legs, heading directly to her brain until she felt her head being penetrated by a thousand chilly darts. Alexis squeezed her ears with both hands.

"You mean rude like not even *looking* at me while we're talking? *That* kind of rude?"

"Come on, Alexis. Check out those guys. See the one in the red shirt?"

"Yeah, I also see his gay lover next to him."

"Jesus, Alexis. Do you have to be so sarcastic?"

Alexis looked over at the duck pond as mother mallard and her ducklings disappeared behind a bend in the pond. She closed her eyes, detecting a low hissing sound like the steady fizzle of a lit fuse ready to ignite.

"So, what do you think?" asked Jody.

"About what?"

"The vomit. I mean, if she throws up in our basement, it must stink to high-heaven, right?"

"Oh, you go down to the basement a lot?"

"Hey, it would leak up through the floor, right?"

Alexis wearily propped her elbows on the table, sinking her face into her open palms, wondering how it was possible to be talking about the status of missing vomit. "I guess she throws up in the toilet," moaned Alexis.

"I don't think so," said Jody.

"What?"

"Did you ever actually *see* her throw up in the toilet?"

"No."

"Did you ever smell puke in the bathroom?"

"No."

"Well," replied Jody, glancing at Alexis, making eye contact for the first time. "You tell me. *Where* does the vomit go?"

"I don't know," groaned Alexis. "Go call the Puke Police."

"Here you are!" exclaimed Sally, setting a Coke in front of Alexis, then scurrying off to another booth.

"Don't be so mean, Alexis," said Jody. "I was just curious about the vomit, that's all."

"Well, it's disgusting and I don't want to think about it. Can we talk about something else for God's sake?"

"You're the one who brought it up."

"Okay, so I brought it up. Now, I'm going to end it once and for all. No more vomit talk, agreed?"

"Sure, but I've seen her too."

"Who?"

"Susie Banford."

"Where? When?"

"I see her going down to the basement all the time."

"Get out of here."

"No really. One time I caught her shoving a Big Mac down her throat. She saw me staring at her and barfed it up. I mean, you talk about *gross.* She looked like a pathetic hooker choking on a blow job."

"Okay Jody. My stomach's doing somersaults. If you mention vomit one more time---"

"Well fine!" cried Jody, tilting her head towards the ceiling and flipping her hair up in a melodramatic display of petulant disappointment. "In that case, I'm leaving!"

Jody jumped up from the booth, heading for the exit, skipping along while waving to everyone, as if she was a stage actress dashing out for an encore. She was almost out the door before Alexis realized the story she told about Susie Banford was pure bullshit.

Five minutes later, Alexis squeezed out of the booth and started walking over to the bar on the other side of the recreation area. Ambling along the olive green carpeting, she spotted four Asian students playing an energetic game of ping pong. The union was beginning to fill up with students returning from classes. Moving towards a throng of incoming students, Alexis suddenly thought they were all gawking at her. A surge of anxiety coursed through her body, convinced that angry judgmental eyes were bearing down on her. In the throes of a vicious panic attack, Alexis felt a wave of self-consciousness so severe she swore she could hear tiny brittle bones creaking in her neck. *How could the bar be so far away?* Staring straight ahead, she pretended she was the mother mallard leading her ducklings to safety.

Finally, she arrived at the bar sweating profusely, trying to remember why on earth she wanted to go to the bar in the first place. She grabbed a stool and took a seat. Jimmy Salamander, the bartender came up to her, flashing a broad smile.

"Hi, Alexis! Whaddaya have?"

"Hi Jimmy. Just a Coke, for now---On second thought, make that a rum and Coke."

"Comin' right up!"

Alexis' thoughts drifted to what she was going to wear to the Hootie and the Blowfish concert on Saturday night. In-between a polarity of decision making about whether to wear black or blue jeans, she spotted Cory Alderman high atop the third floor balcony emerging from the school newspaper office with a black leather case slung over his shoulder. Cory strolled past several student government offices, then descended the blue-tiled steps leading to the main floor. Reaching the bottom of the steps, he paused, looked around, and wiped his collar length, straw-colored hair away from his eyes. Alexis figured he must be going downtown to film something for the newspaper, but he surprised her by turning in her direction. Jimmy placed the rum and Coke in front of her.

"Hi Alexis," said Cory, in a friendly tone.

"Oh, hi Cory!" exclaimed Alexis.

Cory hopped on the stool next to her, slipping the leather case off his shoulder, and placing it on the floor.

"So, how was your summer?" asked Cory.

"Great. I was at the beach."

"I can see you got a tan."

"Yes, but I had to suffer sunburn for over a week! It's my...you know, fair skin...so what did you do all summer?"

"I worked for my town newspaper. Nothing special. Just obits and community affairs stuff. It was pretty boring, but I got some good experience."

Alexis glanced at the leather case on the floor. "Are you doing Sound Bites this year?"

"Yes, I am. In fact, that's why I'm here. Would you like to make a quote?"

"Sure," said Alexis, enthusiastically. "What's the first topic of the year?"

"Well," said Cory, reaching for his camera. "I'm afraid it's not too original. I'm asking people what they did over the summer."

"Oh, no, Cory! I think it's a *great* topic! You can get to the serious stuff later."

Cory stood up, reached down and unzipped the case containing his Sony camcorder. He hoisted the camera on his shoulder, braced it firmly in front of his left eye, squarely facing Alexis. "Boy, I hope there *is* some serious stuff this year. You ready?"

"One second!"

Alexis took a quick sip of her drink, slid off the stool, and ran her hands down her burgundy V-neck sweater, smoothing out the wrinkles, finger combing and fluffing her long wavy chestnut-colored hair. Turning towards the camera, she placed one hand on her hip, striking a theatrical pose while flashing a wide smile. "How do I look, Cory?"

"You look awesome."

"Okay, shoot!" declared Alexis, staring at the tiny red light blinking on the side of the camera.

"Alexis Stewart, what did you do this summer?"

"Oh, I had a wonderful time at the beach in Ocean City working as a waitress in an Italian restaurant. I also read many great novels, and wrote poetry and short stories as part of an independent study for Professor Wilson…"

Following a slight pause, Cory shut off the camera, putting it back in the case. "Thanks, Alexis. You've been a big help. I only need three more."

"Too bad you missed Jody Taylor. She would have been a good person to ask."

"Oh, really?"

"She spent the summer in Iowa working for an acting troupe. I think she got a part in a Shakespearean play."

"Are you and Jody rooming together this year?"

"Yes," replied Alexis, returning to her spot at the bar, and taking another sip. "Jody, Amy and I have an apartment in Lunsford Terrace."

"Amy Toffler?"

"Yes."

"Well," said Cory, "You should have a great year."

"Yeah…we're gonna have a blast."

"It was nice to see you again Alexis. I better find those three other people. I've got a deadline to meet."

"Sure, Cory. Glad to help. When's the paper coming out?"

"Thursday."

"Great. See ya."

"Bye, Alexis."

After she left the student union, Jody went to the cafeteria, walked through the lunch line and took a seat across from Kyle Ransom. She munched on a hamburger and French fries, and sipped a Coke while giving nasty looks to two freshmen hanging out across the room. Staring intently at the women, Jody zoned in on their ersatz combinations of piercings, studs, and tattoos. She couldn't believe the astounding levels of tackiness these bitches were able to achieve. They were so fuckin' desperate for male attention, they'd wear anything—even skimpy, pole-dancing outfits in the middle of November.

She noticed one of them was wearing a powder blue crop top and a pair of Levi's hip huggers she must have lacquered on with a brush. The snotty bitch leaned over into a guy's face, begging her tits to flop out of her top. The angle revealed three tattoos on her back: a rattlesnake crawling up her spine in between two sea green lizards staring bug-eyed at the snake, their long slimy tongues slithering out of their mouths. As if that wasn't enough, she brazenly displayed two gold-plated labret lip rings, a fake diamond nose ring, and a row of tiny multi-colored earrings running up the sides of both ears. The other skankhead wore a round, over-sized gold nose ring, reminding Jody of a hefty prize-winning cow at the county fair.

As she was daydreaming about two beefy cows chewing their cud in a grassy field, she completely forgot that Kyle Ransom had been talking to her. She tried to catch the last part of his sentence, but all she could make out was the word "extreme."

"Oh," said Jody, turning and facing Kyle, "What was extreme, again?"

"Sports, Jody. I was talking about extreme sports. You weren't listening, were you?"

"Well, Kyle, I was distracted. You know, I've got this big part in a movie coming up and I am a bit nervous about it."

"That's okay, it wasn't important."

Jody stared at him, thinking, *No, shit, Sherlock. The only thing extreme around here is boredom, and like dude, you are the fuckin' king of extremely boring.* Jody was about to leave when Kyle unexpectedly caught her attention.

"Hey, Jody, watch out for Sue Terry."

"What? Sue Terry? That nobody?"

"I hear she's spreading ugly rumors about you---telling everyone you slept with Tad Christian."

"Tad Christian! That lousy-as-shit actor? That fuckin' loser? Omygod, he's too short to be a leading man!"

"Hey" said Kyle, grabbing a fry off Jody's plate. "That's what I heard. I thought you might like to know."

"Say Kyle, have you heard about Carlton Weinberg's new movie?"

Kyle looked blankly at Jody, not having the slightest idea who Carlton Weinberg was. He thought he might be the new action hero in *Die Hard*. Kyle was a business major who hated reading, writing, books, classes, and any movie without an arsenal of guns, shootouts and car chases ending in massive destruction. He didn't know anything about films, but he remembered his parents once dragged him to a dreadful, stupid movie called *The Graduate*. He slept through the whole thing.

"Who's Carlton Weinberg?" asked Kyle, reaching over and grabbing another fry.

Jody rolled her eyes to the heavens. "Never mind." Jody realizing she might as well be talking to the bronze statue of Patrick Henry erected in the center of the quad.

"Say," said Kyle, biting a fry in half. "I hear you're rooming with Amy Toffler this year. Is she still going out with that dork Chipper?"

"Yeah, I guess so...among others— Oh! There's Harriet, my neighbor! I need to go over and talk to her! We're taking the same theater course and I need some notes!" Jody threw the rest of her fries on Kyle's tray and bolted from the table. She strutted stiffly past the skanky girls, frowning and tilting her nose in the air, as if she was walking past a barrel of rotting fish. She plopped in a chair next to Harriet who was sitting alone eating a club sandwich and drinking a Mountain Dew.

"Hey, Harriet. Thank God, I saw you! Kyle Ransom is a total fuckin' loser!"

"I know, but he's rich."

"Really? How rich?"

"His old man lights cigars with hundred dollar bills."

"Damn. I should have given him more attention."

"Jesus, you'll never guess. That snotty bitch from Texas---"

"The phony-as-shit one in Deming?"

"Yeah, well she came up to me this morning and pretended to like… be my friend, saying she loved my performance in *The Glass Menagerie* last spring."

"Really?"

"Then she had the nerve to ask me to vote for her because she's running for President of Student Government—not!"

"What did you say?"

"I said, of course Tiffany, no problem! Shit, I wouldn't vote for her if she was running against that Hitler dude."

A group of students entered the cafeteria. Jody and Harriet immediately began a series of snarky comments about each one as if they were judges in a school pageant.

"She's a fuckin' tramp. I heard she slept with a townie."

"I saw that asshole jerking off behind a tree."

"Look at the ugly outfit on that one! Green and orange?"

"He's a hottie. I might have slept with him."

"Him?"

"Maybe not."

"I saw her throwing up in the bathroom."

"Christ, look at her! Pul eeesse…tell me she's not wearing waist-high washed out jeans!"

"God, that's so five minutes ago."

"More like five years."

"No, I threw mine out two years ago."

"At least you threw them out."

After the students disappeared, the girls began discussing the faculty in the theater and film department and how fucked up everybody was. Jody said she thought Bill Bartkowski sucked as a director, but he could act if given the right parts. Harriet thought Alice Prince was probably a lesbian, but not bad as an actress. Jody, feeling a pang of jealousy, said she was okay, but maybe a little *affected* in her delivery. Harriet agreed that Alice could be a bit forced, and wondered why Lyle Frampton never took a shower and talked to himself in the Green Room. Jody said that was because she was crazy. Then Scott Bradshaw cruised by their table, staring at them for a second before getting in line for lunch.

"He's a dick," said Harriet.

"Scott's a dick? I thought he was cool."

"That asshole dumped me at the *Lambda Chi* party for a ditsy freshman who is, like fat... *and* had two abortions."

Jody was going to remind Harriet that she also had two abortions, but what the fuck. "Really? What a prick!"

Jody and Harriet continued their conversation, each of them grasping for something remotely interesting. Harriet said she might go to the Cranberries concert and Jody said she liked them, but they sounded a bit too European, although she had no idea what she meant by European. Then Roy Leavell passed by and Jody noted that he was hot-as-shit, flashing a flirtatious smile that Roy couldn't resist. He circled around and came back to their table and asked how they were doing. Jody quickly perked up and told him about getting the part in Psycho *Sorority Drug Ring*.

Roy heard that Jody gave terrific blow jobs so he pretended to care about her acting career. Jody thought Harriet was jealous because Roy talked to her most of the time, but she was surprised when Roy left after a few minutes saying he had a tennis match with Christian Rawlings, a notorious gay dude, making Jody wonder if Roy was gay, or bi, or whatever.

Harriet, totally bored, stood up to leave, but Amy Toffler abruptly burst into the cafeteria, prancing along on balls of her feet like a show horse, flashing a beaming, petrified smile to everyone, as if she was Jackie Kennedy riding in a parade with her husband.

"Hey guys! What's going on?" squealed Amy, strutting up to Jody and Harriet, plunking down in a chair, and beating on the table like it was a drum set. Jody cupped her palms to her ears, as if ice pick pierced her brain. "Amy, plu...ease! I have a headache."

"Gee, are you okay?"

"Sure, Amy. I'm just not in the mood for a daytime drum solo."

Amy stopped drumming, then finger-combed her long blonde hair out of her face. "So, what's up with you guys?"

Jody and Harriet glanced at each other.

Jody thinking, *I see before me a cute, trained circus pony. I'm dying to ask her to count to three by stomping her left foot.*

Harriet thinking, *I wonder why no one has grabbed a knife and cut her tongue out.*

"Hey Amy," asked Jody, "Do you know if Roy Leavell is gay or not?"

"Of course he is. He came out last year. Why?"

"Nothing. Forget it."

Amy began chattering on about the fall formal, announcing that she was going with Chipper and what she was going to wear, and who the band was going to be, and how Chipper was going to rent a limousine and on and on, ignoring the stabbing stares from Jody who was fighting off the urge to plunge a fork between her boob-job big tits. Harriet glared at Amy with loathing-laced eyes, silently begging her to please-please-please-shut-the-fuck-up. She considered interrupting her to tell her she didn't give a flying fuck about the formal because she decided on Thursday to become a lesbian. Non-verbal cues were wasted on Amy who launched into another high-pitched, rapid, staccato monologue informing the girls about what happened on *Melrose Place* last night, new books about personal growth, a brand new lavender body wash, and the healthy benefits of early morning workouts. Jody squeezed her left ear, checking to see if it was bleeding.

Amy paused, took a deep breath, and before Jody and Harriet could find a way to disappear, she asked them what they were going to do over the weekend. Jody told her she was busy shooting the film in Boston. Harriet lied, saying she was going out with James Carrington, a moronic soccer player who once had sex with a girl on the President's lawn, then threw the used condom on his porch. She did not want Amy to know she had become a lesbian on Thursday and she was really going to attend a gay sorority party and hit on Emily Bergamo, a rich, but not too snotty, sophomore from Selma, Alabama. Jody grabbed her chance to escape when she saw Carl Weldon in the smoking section, talking to a freaky-looking, horrorshow freshman.

"Hey, guys, I need to see Carl Weldon over there. He's in my Plays and Performance class."

As Jody stood up to leave, Amy was prattling on about a book called *Men Who Can't Love.* Harriet remained perfectly still. She wished she had a mirror to see if she looked like one of those bug-eyed stiffs found frozen in a glacier for a thousand years.

As Jody approached Carl, she got a better look at the skanky freshman who was obscenely dressed in a too-tight canary yellow sweater, pink paisley leggings, and a pair of alligator-skinned boots. She had scraggly, bleached-blonde hair with dark roots showing, and sporting a hideous purple nose ring. Her thin, pointy face was caked with dust-colored makeup highlighted by thin lips smeared with fuck-me-red lipstick. Jody thought Carl must have lost his mind.

"Hey, big boy," she moaned. "How about giving a poor girl a cigarette?"

"Sure," said Carl, reaching into his shirt pocket for a Marlboro Light.

The freshman gave Jody a nasty smirk, controlling her urge to grab a knife and stab it into this bitch's face. Carl handed Jody a cigarette, then lit it with a Bic lighter.

"Thanks, dah...ling," Jody cooed, "You are soooo....mau...velous. Why don't you come up and see me sometime?"

Carl somehow restrained from laughing in her face, eyeing the freshman who placed both hands on her hips while glaring at Jody as if she just farted. Jody felt a surge of self-fulfillment, thinking her Southern belle accent was perfect and hoping she could use it in the film. She took a slow, melodramatic drag off her cigarette, flitting her eyelashes at Carl, then blew a huge plume of smoke into the freshman's face. Carl never heard a more ridiculous, phony accent in his life and wondered what Jody really wanted. He had already made arrangements to take out the freshman and fuck her brains out. Jody could tell Carl was impressed with her dramatic flair and knew he wanted to ditch this ditsy chick. She leaned over and whispered in his ear, telling him to meet her at the union at ten o'clock. Carl nodded affirmatively, giving the impression that he would actually show up. Jody scrutinized the freshman, slowly sizing her up from head to toe, then considered asking her which carnival she bought her makeup from.

"Well, dah...ings, I have to run now. Ya'll be good boys and girls! My adorable fans are waiting!" Jody flicked her cigarette in the air, then skipped back to the girl's table and sat down.

Harriet had nodded off, her head drooping into the palm of her hand. In spite of Harriet being unconscious, Amy was still gushing effusively, informing Harriet what she was going to do this weekend, then shifted in mid-sentence to raving about the greatness of the Bangles, declaring with great confidence that they were better than New Kids on the Block.

"No kidding!" screamed Jody, loud enough to wake up Harriet.

Harriet quickly opened her eyes, staring at Jody with a mixture of shock and confusion. "Huh…I gotta go," muttered Harriet. "My…huh… mother's going to call me."

"Wait!" yelled Amy. "What's the best soap? I've got to know!"

"Soap?" asked Jody.

"Yes! Look at my hands! They're all dried out!"

Harriet sunk her head into her hands. "Okay I gotta go, but try Almay—it's good for sensitive skin."

Jody quickly faced Harriet. "Almay? That's *my* soap."

"What do you mean *my* soap?" asked Harriet.

"Well, I mean… like when did *you* use Almay?"

"I don't fuckin' remember. What's your point?"

"Well…never mind. It's just I don't like people using my soap."

"So, nobody can buy Almay but you? Or are you accusing me of using your fuckin' soap?"

"No, not at all," lied Jody

"There she is!" cried Amy. "It's the vomit girl!"

"Omygod, it's Queen Yack!"

"Patty Puke!"

The girls stared at a tall, thin, statuesque student with large round eyes, prominent cheek bones, and long, straight blonde hair cascading down the length of her back. She was carrying a salad to a table.

"Yeah, that's her," said Amy.

A pregnant pause engulfed the table. Then Amy filled the dead air. "I think Lou Carter has a small penis."

Immediately, Jody and Harriet responded in unison: "How do you know?!"

Amy, nonplussed said, "I heard it from a freshman."

Jody thought it was a pretty good lie for someone as dumb as Amy. Harriet followed the remark by noting that Sarah Crews had probably slept with a hundred guys. "You mean Sarah Screws?" blurted Jody. Harriet said she thought Joe Tyson might be gay or bi. Amy agreed and said she saw him dancing the Latin hustle this summer with a surfer dude in a gay nightclub called *Gatsby's*. Jody said she thought Tonya Small had herpes because she saw her with a gross blister on her lip. After another uncomfortable pause, the threesome ran out of energy and people to talk about.

Later in the afternoon Alexis entered the apartment and spotted Amy lying on the sofa watching TV. She was lounging in a pair of pink flannel pajamas, looking tired and pale, like a stale powdered donut.

"Hey, Amy," said Alexis, "Guess what? I did a Sound Bite for Cory Alderman."

"Yeah? What did he ask you?"

"What I did over the summer."

"Sounds boring."

"Really? Are you saying I'm boring?"

Amy slowly uncoiled her body, stretching her left arm towards the coffee table struggling to reach the remote. She grunted like a weightlifter, grasping the device before falling back on the couch, emitting muted childlike moaning sounds. "No, Alexis. Of course you're not boring. It's the topic. I mean, who cares?"

"Right. Who the fuck cares?" muttered Alexis, marching towards her bedroom.

"Wait!" cried Amy. "There might be something good on."

Alexis stopped, curious to find out what Amy could possibly find on TV worth watching. Standing in the middle of the room, Alexis glowered at her roommate while she channel surfed through a myriad of TV offerings, pointing and clicking every couple seconds, apparently unable to find anything to her liking.

Standing motionless, Alexis became mesmerized by the dizzy parade of mind-numbing drivel flashing before her eyes, assaulting her senses, like a deafening Metallica video. Then, as if mind-controlled by Amy's remote, she plopped down on a padded chair across from the TV, continuing to ogle intently at a barrage of trashy talk shows, sit-com reruns, infomercials, soap operas, and silly game shows that were given their allotted two seconds of attention.

Finally, Amy's careening, circuitous search for a suitable show landed on *The Oprah Winfrey Show*. Alexis felt a surge of anger, hoping it would not escalate into uncontrollably fury as she sat dumbfounded trying to figure out how anyone could be addicted to the omnipresent banality of modern life.

"Goldie Hawn's on *Oprah*," announced Amy.

"Again?"

Amy was obsessed with talk shows, Diet Cokes, her boyfriend Chipper, cheating on Chipper, the mirror, *Melrose Place,* kinky sex, Clinique skincare toner, *Buns of Steel* work-out videos, anything sold at *Victoria's Secret,* and her daily horoscope in the newspaper.

"I wish she'd just marry Kurt Russell," noted Amy.

"What?"

"Goldie Hawn. She should marry Kurt Russell. I think they really love each other."

"Right…"

Amy continued, "I think Goldie's more mature than her *Laugh-In* days."

"What? Goldie Hawn, mature? Come on, Amy. She's a washed-up blond bimbo. Shit, *Laugh-In* was the best thing she ever did."

"Well, I think you're wrong," replied Amy, folding her arms tightly around her chest. Watching Amy's vacant eyes glued intensely to *Oprah,* Alexis concluded that they would undoubtedly kill each other before the year was out.

"Are you going to the Hootie and the Snowfish concert tomorrow night?" asked Amy.

Alexis audibly sighed. "Blowfish Amy…It's Blowfish, for God's sake."

"Whatever. Are you going?"

"Yes, but I need something to wear."

Suddenly, Jody Taylor swung open the front door, charging in dramatically like an excitable winner running down the aisle to pick up her Oscar. Checking herself furtively in the mirror, she launched into an earnest primping session, adjusting her green knit pullover, shaking her vermilion red hair from side-to-side, rubbing makeup on one cheek, and smoothing out her fiery red lipstick with her fingertips. For an instant, she frowned at the mirror as if disappointed with the results, then quickly recovered. Waving her arms above her head and springing in the air, she yelled, "Did you tell them about the part!"

Alexis said, "We're very excited for you."

"Hey, what are you watching?" asked Jody.

"Oprah," said Amy. "Goldie's on."

"Is Kurt Russell going to be on?" asked Jody.

"I don't think so," said Amy."

"Omygod," declared Jody. "He's hot-as-shit—and he's got a big dick."

"What?" asked Alexis, suddenly paying attention. "He's a dick?"

"No, no," replied Jody. "I said, I bet he has a *big* dick."

"Really? How can you tell?"

"He just looks like he's got one, that's all."

Alexis tried to think what Kurt Russell looked like. *Was he the one in Die-Hard? Maybe he was the one in Pretty Woman. What about that guy in Dirty Dancing?*

"Alexis did a Sound Bite for Cory Alderman this afternoon," said Amy, who like Alexis was not interested in discussing the size of Kurt Russell's penis.

"Oh," said Jody, "What did he ask you?"

"What I did this summer."

"Cool. What did you tell him?"

"I told him all about my study with Tom."

"Shit, Alexis, is that legal?"

"What do you mean *legal?*"

"Alexis, you're sleeping with him. Isn't that against the rules?"

"No—and it's none of your business, anyway."

"You're the one who brought it up."

"Actually Jody   oh, never mind!"

"I'm getting my haircut tomorrow," Jody said to the mirror.

"Short?" asked Amy.

"Not!" cried Jody. "I'll just have Rudy take a few inches off. I need to look good for this movie. Remember, if a girl needs a haircut, she may need a shave!"

Alexis arched her back, twisted around in her chair, gaping at Jody making love to the mirror. Alexis had to admit that Jody was probably the most attractive woman on campus. She was tall and thin and blessed with naturally curly, shoulder-length flaming red hair, and dazzling crystal ice-blue eyes that glistened brilliantly when the stage lights struck her. Her complexion was nearly flawless, except for a tiny dotting of freckles sprinkled across the bridge of her nose and cheeks.

Jody gave the mirror one more approving look, and then retired to her room. Alexis glanced at the TV noticing that *Oprah* had been replaced by one of the Brady Bunch girls having an argument with one of their brothers about who was going to move into the newly renovated room in the attic. Abruptly, Alexis jumped up from the chair, striding briskly towards her bedroom, but before she reached the door, Amy called out to her, "Hey! Katrina and the Waves are playing at Trax and the *Zete* guys are having a party afterwards! You wanna go?"

"No, thanks. Is Chipper going to be there?"

"No, he's going to some stupid kickboxing thing."

Alexis opened the bedroom door, turning back to Amy. "What do you think I should wear to the Hootie and the Blowfish concert?"

"Oh, go casual. Just wear jeans and a sweater. All their fans dress like slobs. You'll be overdressed if you wear something nice."

"Yeah," muttered Alexis, just before closing the door. "I guess you're right. I'll find something."

Alexis plopped down on her bed, took a few deep breaths, assuming an angel-in-the-snow position. She lay motionless, trying to revive her depleted energy, her left handcasually draped over the side of the bed. After a few minutes relaxing and gazing at the ceiling, she imagined blood dripping from her fingertips down to the floor. She thought it was stupid to look and see if blood was actually trickling out her body, but the sensation wouldn't go away. In spite of herself, she lifted her head, raised her hand, and inspected her fingers as if admiring freshly painted nails. Relieved at seeing bloodless fingers, she smiled ruefully, then lay back on the bed.

Without warning, Amy came bounding in the room like Spiderman wired on speed, jumping up and down on her bed, waving her arms frenetically while performing a series of maniacal aerobic exercises. A stunned Alexis glared at her as Amy screamed, '1-2-3-1; 1-2-3-2; 1-2-3-3!' Alexis rushed towards her, grabbed her legs, and tackled her on the bed, sending them flying through the air before crashing their heads bluntly against the headboard.

"That's enough!" cried Alexis. "I'm a not in the mood for your goddamn silly workout routine—especially on my bed! Jesus Christ! Five minutes ago you were half-dead on the sofa!"

"Gosh, Alexis, I'm sorry!" cried Amy, rolling over to the side of the bed, rubbing her bruised forehead. "What's with you? Why you stressing? You trying to kill me, or something?"

Alexis leaned forward, bracing her back with a pillow, her head already aching from the blow. "Nothing...forget it. I was just...you know...busy. Can't you *knock,* or something?"

"Okay, no problem. I'm sorry. I just thought you might want to see the newest *Buns of Steel* workout. It's awesome."

"Maybe later on..."

"Am I getting a bruise?" asked Amy, pushing her hair back to reveal a slight redness on her forehead.

"No, it's nothing. Sorry. I guess I don't know my own strength."

Amy nodded, shrugged her shoulders, and then nonchalantly got up from the bed, strode over to Alexis' closet and started rummaging through her clothes.

"Looking for something?" asked Alexis.

"I need an outfit for tonight."

"Don't pick the blue sweater. It's new. Come on Amy, you have a whole closet full of clothes."

"These are too big," announced Amy, holding up a pair of gray slacks.

"What do you mean too *big?*"

Amy's eyes roamed dejectedly over a rumpled pile of clothes lying on the floor as if they were damaged goods at the Salvation Army. "I think you're a size bigger than me. Do you have any black leggings?"

"No."

"Maybe I should wear a skirt and blouse."

"Don't touch the paisley one. It's too nice."

"Did you decide what to wear to the Hootie and the Crowfish concert?" Amy asked, tossing a silk lavender blouse on the bed.

"Blowfish! Not Crowfish!"

"Whatever...who gives a shit. I mean Hootie gives a shit!" Amy laughed at her own joke. Alexis, in spite of herself, smiled at the enormous absurdity of it all. Amy may be an idiot, but at least she was a transparent one.

"No," said Alexis. "I don't know what I'm wearing to the concert. I'm so *big,* you know. I'll see if I can find an elephant who is selling his old clothes at a yard sale."

"Hey, Alexis. I'm sorry. That didn't come out right. I didn't mean to say you were fat, or anything."

"I know. Don't worry about it."

"Hey, why don't you come with me? We're gonna have a lot of fun."

"No thanks. Those guys at *Zete* are a bunch of dicks."

"I know. But it's free beer and I'm gonna get wasted."

"Go for it."

"Is this alright?" asked Amy, displaying a pair of green print leggings with a bulky L.L. Bean tan knit sweater. In spite of the over-sized look, Amy's gorgeous figure was still distinctly noticeable. Alexis had to admit she looked fabulous. "Yeah, you look fine. Go get 'em. By the way, when are you going to see Chipper again?"

"Next weekend. We're going to the Pixies concert."

"Never heard of them."

"You're kidding."

All of a sudden, Alexis detected a perceptible change in the room's temperature. It seemed much hotter. A sickening odor permeated the atmosphere, as if the vile stench from Oriental corpse flowers was ascending from the basement. Her lungs felt like they were on fire and she clutched her throat, choking and gasping for breath. In a panic, she rolled over on the bed, wrapped a pillow around her arms, her stomach churning inside as she wheezed and coughed repeatedly into the pillow. The ceiling spun around in violent, spiraling circles. *Did Amy bring something into the room? What's happening here?*

Amy stood frozen in place watching Alexis, unsure what to do. Then, she snapped out of it, rushing to her side. "Alexis, are you alright? Can I get you something?"

"What…?"

"A glass of water? Anything?"

"Yes, please!"

Amy ran quickly into the kitchen, but by the time she returned, Alexis was passed out cold.

A week had gone by since Alexis passed out in her bedroom. Entering the apartment she tilted her head, sniffing the air like a curious bunny rabbit, convinced there was whiff of the noxious odor the air. She wondered why the odd smell created a vague sense of uneasiness and bodily discomfort, not just physically, but mentally as well. She couldn't help but think her roommates had something to do with it.

Alexis sat on the couch and turned on the TV. As she was channel surfing, Jody emerged from her bedroom, looking tired and dragged out, eating a cookie and carrying a Diet Coke.

"What's for dinner?" asked Jody.

"I think it's some kind of chicken casserole."

"Gross, let's go out."

"Where?"

"I don't know. How about Spanky's?"

"Alright. Should we wait for Amy?"

"No, she's been getting on my nerves. I'm tired of her."

"I'll leave her a note."

"Okay."

Alexis and Jody entered Spanky's and walked over to the antique cherry booths lining the perimeter of the restaurant adjacent to the bar. The booths were empty except for a young couple at the closest end listening to a bouncy tune playing on a nearby jukebox. The two women strolled past them to the far end and chose the last booth. As they sat down, Alexis looked at Jody, but she was already focused on something behind her. Alexis glanced over her shoulder, spotting a large mirror. Immediately, Jody launched into her routine, checking out the condition of her hair, lipstick, and makeup.

"I hope we get a hot waiter," Jody said to the mirror.

Momentarily, a young, thin waiter in a white shirt, black vest, and maroon bow-tie arrived to take their order. As if sprung into action by a director's cue, Jody perked up, assuming a theatrical pose, quickly lighting a cigarette, and flashing her wide blue eyes.

"Ready to order?" he asked.

"Yes, dah…ling," Jody moaned seductively, "I'll take a hamburger and a Budweiser."

Alexis wanted to evaporate. "I'll take a cheeseburger, French fries, and a Coors Light."

The waiter left. After a brief pause, Alexis gave in to the inevitable. "So, how are the scenes going?"

"Okay, but the leading guy hasn't shown up yet, so we're using a stand-in."

"Who is he?

"His name is James Duncan. He's done some low budget stuff and some commercials. I heard he's hot-as-shit."

Cory Alderman entered the restaurant carrying his camcorder.

"There's Cory Alderman," said Alexis.

Jody looked furtively in Cory's direction, then back to the mirror, shrugging slightly, "He needs a haircut."

"I like longer hair."

"Isn't he, like older?"

"He might be, but I think he's a pretty good student. He's not a dumb frat guy, that's for sure. Maybe he'll ask you to do a Sound Bite."

"I hope he does. I will tell everybody about the film."

Cory appeared to be looking for someone. Then he spotted the two women and came over to their table. "Hi, Alexis. How's it going?"

"Great. Do you know Jody Taylor?"

"No, nice to meet you."

"Would you like to join us?" asked Alexis.

"Sure."

Cory sat down next to Alexis, placing his leather case next to him. He glanced at Jody, who was looking at herself put on more lipstick.

"Aren't you a theater major?" he asked.

Jody immediately turned away from the mirror. "Why, yes. It's the theater *and* film department. Have you seen me?"

"No, but I heard you're very good."

"Thanks," said Jody, her mood warming. "We have a great department. Are you going to do a Sound Bite in here?"

"No, thank goodness I'm done for the day."

The young waiter arrived with the orders. Cory asked for a cheeseburger and a Heineken. After the waiter left, he began talking about his political theory class, mentioning the Iran-Contra affair. Jody and Alexis did their best to keep up with the conversation. Jody's attention wandered back and forth between the mirror and Cory's comments about President Reagan's chances of maintaining his high standings in the polls..."But he might have trouble if the budget problems continue..."

Alexis took a sip of her beer, staring at Cory.

"Oh, I don't think the budget will be a problem, do you?"

"I think it might be," said Cory, seriously. "The deficit has been rising and he might have to increase taxes."

"There's Jody!" screamed Amy.

Amy Toffler glided into Spanky's like a Hollywood actress making love to the *paparazzi.* She was dressed to the nines, decked out in a green stretch spandex mini-dress with spaghetti straps, hip-belted leggings, glass shoulder duster earrings, and high black leather boots.

"Hi guys!" squealed Amy, sliding in the booth next to Jody. "Guess what?"

"What?" asked everyone, including Cory.

"I joined the *Sassy* club!"

Alexis and Jody flashed each other conspiratorial glances.

Cory asked, "Is that a club on campus?"

"No Cory," said Alexis. "The *Sassy* club is the name of a club in a magazine."

"*Sassy* is a magazine?" asked Cory.

"Yes," responded Alexis. "It's a magazine like *Cosmopolitan,* only for younger people, like high school students."

"No it isn't!" blurted Amy. "It's for high school *and* college students—and I'm glad I joined the club!"

Cory asked, "What do they do in the club?"

"You don't do anything," interjected Alexis. "All they do is send you bunches of junk, like a questionnaire to find out who you think is the sassiest boy in America, or give you vital information like Christian Slater's nickname is 'Thumper.'"

"That's not true!" shouted Amy. "They have serious articles on the Middle East and air pollution, and stuff! You're just jealous!"

"Oh sure," said Alexis. "I'm jealous because you joined a club that takes everybody who sends them twenty-five bucks."

Amy slumped back in the booth, folded her arms, sealing her lips. Jody remained thoroughly nonplussed having been through these bouts of triviality countless times. She was more focused on the waiter with the vest and bow-tie, wondering if was available. Cory remained silent. Alexis knew she had to change Amy's mood, or she would ruin it for everybody.

"Hey, Amy. I'm sorry. Let's forget the whole thing. I love *Sassy!*"

Then the conversation shifted to familiar territory—talking about how cheesy the freshmen were. Amy said Loretta Bunson was a loud pee-er because she heard her in a bathroom at a frat party. Jody laughed and said they should record her peeing and play it over the loud speakers at the next *Phi Delt* party. Jody, now on a manic roll, told a gross cafeteria story about a retarded-as-shit freshman with tangled mousy brown hair poking her dirty, grimy fingers through the plastic wrap of a cheeseburger, making mooing sounds as she did it. The other two girls screamed, "Moo! Moo!" like drunken cows in a field. Amy, laughing hysterically, began telling everyone about the latest issue of *Sassy* which had pictures of very hot guys from Beverly Hills 90210 posing in their underwear. Jody immediately said something gross about skid marks and the other girls yelled, "Yuck!" Then, Alexis chortled like a hyena, blurting out, "Wow, can I become a member of the *Sassy* Club? I heard it's, like awesome!" Then, Jody hollered, "Look! There's the vomit girl!" They all glared at the slim blonde girl from the cafeteria who came in and sat at the bar while the girls made disgusting comments about her anorexia and bulimia, and then Jody asked, "What does she do with the vomit?" and Alexis immediately cried, "Why do you always ask that question?" Jody responded, "I don't know," and they all three started to laugh and giggle like three little school girls and ordered a pitcher of beer and now all of them were flirting with the hot young waiter while making more vomit jokes, remarking what a bunch of dicks the guys at *Theta* were, and then more beers came, the girls chugging them down like there was no tomorrow, and at one point Jody asked where Cory Alderman was and they all looked around, figuring he must have left because they didn't see him anywhere.

# Solitary Eyes on Fire

Todd Benjamin was having trouble distinguishing MTV from the Book of Revelation. Relaxing in his girlfriend Leslie Richards apartment in Charlottesville, Virginia, he was almost prone, slouching down in a big blue recliner staring pie-eyed at the screen wondering if the Apostle John was going to appear in the next video. Nearby an electric fireplace hissed and sizzled at him, giving him more creeps than the TV, sounding an arrogant pissed-off rattlesnake bugging him for attention. He was drinking a beer, popping Percocets and Darvons, the low steady droning of Leslie's hairdryer buzzing in from the bathroom, disturbing and confusing his ears. Todd thinking, *I don't know why, but the whirring noise gets on my nerves….reminds me of my life right now.*

Suddenly, ZZ Top flashed on the screen, swinging their guitars with six video vixens in Daisy Duke shorts prancing on the bright red hood of a pimped-out hot rod Ford, screaming electric guitars detonating from the tube. Todd thought they were singing about legs, but he wasn't sure.

Leslie opened the bathroom door clutching her hair dryer, bending over and aggressively swinging her long flowing auburn hair from side-to-side like a singer in an 80's hair band. Wearing only black lace panties and a matching bra, she pushed her hair back with a swift hand motion, rising up and glancing in the mirror. Excited and aroused at the sight, Todd tried hoisting himself out of the chair, but fell backwards, spilling his beer…

*Oh the hell with it…don't feel like going to the trouble right now. Besides, she might be the ancient harlot garbed in purple and scarlet, adorned with gold and pearls. I believe the earthly dirges have lamented the loss of ordained purity, and thus, the end of music. Video is over and some DJ is announcing the next MTV theme of the week. Ohmygod, John, he said, totally serious that they are conducting a Madonnathon with 100 of her hideous heathen videos.*

*Makes me want to put a gun to my head. But I know I have to accept the hard life, to deal with outright stupor, close the coffin lid and suffocate. I hear the voice of the great multitude in my head, the sound of many waters, and mighty thunder peals. Is it not time for the end of Satan's evil reign? Damn, spilled my beer...got to get to the kitchen....Uh, Billy Idol is jumping up and down on a bed while a young hardbody is crawling across the floor, like a panther in heat, stalking some preppy nerd. Girl is hot, but she will not be here for the resurrection. I think perhaps she should have the mark on her forehead, or hands like the rest of the martyrs who will surely be cast into the lake of fire with the rest of the harlots, shores, and thieves...*

Leslie emerged from the bedroom dressed in casual faded jeans and a red pullover. She was a slender, smooth-skinned beauty with high cheek bones, full red lips, and sparkling almond-shaped hazel eyes. Blessed with long sinuous legs, she moved through space with the effortless fluidity of a ballet dancer. She approached Todd, leaned over the back of his chair, and gave him a long slow kiss on the lips.

"You look great," said Todd.

"Thanks. Was it worth the wait?"

"Are you kidding? Want to watch the Madonnathon?"

"Very funny."

Leslie eased her way around the chair, playfully toppling on Todd's lap. She gazed up at Todd, her eyes narrowing, brows furrowing, and lips tightening. "Todd, I want you to know that I am here for you if you need me."

"What do you mean?"

"Those drugs. They're ruining your personality. You are drifting off... more and more..."

"I'm okay."

"Promise me you will lay off those awful pills—and whatever else you are taking."

"I promise. I think you're right. They do strange things to my head."

"I'll be right back. I need to call my dad. Are you okay?"

"Sure, right as rain..."

*...a chill in the air...singer comes on MTV who is actually uglier than Billy Idol. Christ, he's wearing a T-shirt with a slice of lemon pie splashed across the front...Light a joint, pop a couple Percocets...find myself drifting listlessly into*

*the kitchen to grab a Bud from the fridge…..only have two left…return to the living room…nothing happening…go into the bedroom and look in on Leslie who is talking to a sinner on the phone. Or perhaps she is talking to the great multitude. Wandering around the apartment…everything empty. Flipping through a Cosmopolitan magazine, or maybe it's a Watchtower. Floating back in my chair…Percents soaking up my brain…oozing in a state of rubbery consciousness… sprinkle some angel dust on a joint, light it, and wander off to Jerusalem. MTV and the apocalypse are calling me. My eyes heavy-lidded, half-mast, droopy, and drowsy. What? Perchance to dream and fill this void? A dull fix of the mind? This is the blood that makes the outlaws. I have been of an inferior race forever. I understand a new epoch is at hand, bursting with sordid terror. What low and vile nature is about to commence? Modernity is the peasant's grasp of the world untouched by miracles.*

Leslie emerged from the bedroom, walking briskly towards Todd, a handbag in her hand.

"He's okay," she said.

"He's okay?"

"My dad, silly. Did you forget he's in the hospital?"

"No, of course not."

"Listen honey, I need to go to the drugstore to pick up some feminine products. I'll be right back, okay?"

"Sure, no problem."

"Are you sure you're alright? You look a little distant."

"I'm right as rain in Spain…in the membrane."

"I won't take long."

"Are you sure you're okay?"

"No prob…limo"

Okay, bye," said Leslie, kissing Todd on the cheek.

Todd slumped further into his chair. He looked to see if Leslie had left and when he turned his head back the hallucinations more vivid, the TV suddenly walking towards him on thin, snake-like legs protruding from its base, flashing hideous, kaleidoscopic, and threatening images…

*…hard to describe, but videos are becoming more symbolic, more violent. I see "The Anti-Christ is coming" peeking out of the box. Almost hit me…I don't deserve to see two olive trees and three broken lampshades talking to*

*Downtown Julie Brown which is very confusing if you ask me. I must refrain from lonesome soliloquies, evil intentions.*

*I turn around, hearing strange crisp, snapping sounds of flip-flops flapping snap along the wooden floor like polite clapping at a Russian ballet. Flapping little echoes dissipating up the stairs, a gentle song fading into stillness. Slowly, irrevocably melting into rubbery consciousness. Is this all about transmutation? This must be the blood that makes the outlaw. I'm sure there are lots of messages coming out that I should be paying attention to. The Antichrist is coming!" is bursting from the screen again. When are we going to witness the judgments and punishments of the harlots? It's an ancient agreement, right? I must avoid glimpses of the pseudo-divine essence, erotic flowers, drowsy melodies from ancient scribes. Another video appears. This time, it is an old woman clothed with only the sun to protect her, the yellow moon under her feet, a crown of twelve stars piercing her graying head, singing, "Any day now, I shall be released."*

Leslie returned from the store, finding Todd passed out in his chair, a can of Budweiser still clutched in his hand.

"Todd! Wake up, it's me! Time to go out, lover boy."

Todd slowly came to life, took a swig of beer, and then wiped his face with the sleeve of his other hand.

"How long have I been out?" he asked.

"Not long. I was only gone for a half-hour." You ready?"

"Sure. Where are we going?"

"Jake's Tavern, silly. Did you forget that we're meeting the guys tonight? You want them to get another drummer?"

"Hell, no. Let's go."

Todd attempted to extract himself from the chair, but he fell backwards, striking his head against the cushion.

"Are you okay" asked Leslie. "You want me to get you something?"

"No, I'm all right. Give me a few minutes. I'm feeling a little woozy."

"Woozy? Jesus, Todd, you're lucky to be alive. You're lucky you're feeling *anything* with all the shit you've been drinking and popping."

"That's me...a popping drinker...a drunken pooper...a drunken pt... able...a...hole."

"Jesus Christ," screamed Leslie, flinging her handbag towards the fireplace, knocking over a set of andirons before storming into the bedroom. Todd sat immobilized...

*...I look again at MTV and see nothing but filth and vermin at the end of an all-night souse. Yahweh's war bow flashes like lightning, sparkling jaspers, carnelian emeralds, sapphires and diamonds, stones of paradise, blinding me.*

*Another dimension. Pales and trembles slumping into unfathomable abyss...A frightful smile appears, then disappears down the boulevard of broken dreams. Ether-beaten old bums, crusty old crones languishing on MTV. I have certain unsustainable deficiencies...Why else would the waters of my forgotten ancestors leave me beached along the silent, aching shore? Screen suddenly blurs, metabolizing into celluloid breakdown, images of color liquefaction go blobbing along, oozing slime, molting into blood-boiled plasma.*

Leslie waited an hour before coming out of the bedroom.

"Todd?" she asked, leaning over the chair to see if Todd was conscious.

"Yes?"

"You passed out."

"Sorry, honey. What time is it?"

"Ten o'clock."

"Not to late for Jake's, right?"

"Sure, if you still want to go."


Todd and Leslie walked into Jake's tavern, momentarily blinded by the dimly lit establishment.

"Christ," said Todd, "It's darker than angelica night."

The couple wandered over to an ageless mahogany bar reminiscent of western movies, a blackened, boot-heeled brass rail rimming the bottom of the bar. Leslie followed Todd to the center of the bar. They sat on stools, sizing up the choices on tap, Old Milwaukee, Budweiser, and Coors light, labeled on long sturdy wooden-handles. Seated next to them were two crusty old men identically dressed in red plaid flannel shirts and bib overalls. Bleary-eyed and sullen, they rotated their heads towards Todd and Leslie in perfect unison, like robots on remote control.

"With no bartender in sight, Todd yelled, "Anybody home!"

Jake, the bartender was perched on a stool at the end of the bar hiding his face in a newspaper. Dropping the newspaper, he shouted, "Hey Todd, What's your hurry? Going somewhere important?"

"Yeah, Jake," cried Todd, "I'm sitting in for Ringo Starr tonight at Shea Stadium."

Jake slowly meandered down the bar. "Good evening, Leslie, What can I get for you?"

"I'll have a Coors Light."

"Great. And you, Mr. Krupa."

"Who?"

"Never mind, sonny. Waddaya have?"

"Gimme a Bud, old fart."

Jake poured the couple their beers.

"Hey Jake, Where are the guys?"

"I think they're fighting out back."

"Again?" muttered Leslie.

"I don't know Leslie," said Jake, shrugging. "I guess they don't have anything better to do."

Todd scanned the tavern, looking for his friends. In the rear of the bar, the usual gang of stoners, bikers, greasers, and locals were hanging out, drinking beer, and shooting pool. The whole scene depressed Todd, feeling as if he was the biggest loser in a townie bar for losers. "I don't see them," he mumbled, staring fixedly at a crooked "Buy or Bye Bye" sign taped on the wall at the end of the bar.

"Do you think they're really fighting?" asked Leslie.

"I'll check it out, said Todd. "Stay here."

Todd strode towards the back entrance, but before he reached the door Billy, Chris, and Dutch unexpectedly burst through the door like scrambling soldiers fleeing incoming mortars.

"Holy shit!" cried Billy. "We beat the crap outta those motherfuckers! Did you see them run like scared jackrabbits!"

"Fickin'-A," screamed Chris. "They ran like pussy rabbits!"

"I know I broke that asshole's jaw!" hollered Dutch, waving his arms, vigorously throwing air punches and jabs at an unseen opponent.

"Whoa!" cried Todd, "Who did you fight?"

Billy slumped into a booth, exhausted, trying to catch his breath. "It was...whew...Joey Culbertson and his gay fuckin' friends. We cleaned their clocks!"

"Poor Joey's got garbage for dinner now," said Chris, sliding into the booth and pushing Billy against the wall.

"Garbage for dinner? How's that?" asked Todd.

Dutch flopped in the booth across from to Billy and Chris. "Yeah, said Dutch, grinning from ear-to-ear, "Joey said Billy smelled like tobacco spit, so Billy kicked his ass, then made him eat garbage from one of the dumpsters out back. It was awesome."

Todd squeezed into the booth next to Dutch. Billy motioned to Jake to bring a round of beers while Leslie who had been watching the whole scene came over to join them.

"Well fellas," said Leslie, taking a seat next to Todd. "It sounds like you all just won Olympic gold medals."

"Yeah," said Dutch. "The gold metal for ass-kicking!"

"Shit," muttered Billy. "It was nothing. Just another day at the office."

Chris turned to Todd and Leslie. "So what have you guys been up to?"

"Nothing much," said Leslie. "I'm still going to community college and slaving away at Rosie's."

"The diner?" asked Billy.

"Yes, four nights a week. It sucks."

"Better than the Anti-Christ factory," said Todd, gazing languidly in the distance, a devilish, stoned-out look spreading across his face.

"And that means, what?" asked Dutch, incredulously.

"Nothing," said Todd. "I gotta go see...something...uh...someone..."

"Christ, Todd," moaned Billy. What the fuck is up with you? You've been sounding strange lately—even for us."

"I'm okay," said Todd. "I'm just going through this nothing-means-shit-to-me phase."

"Thanks, said Leslie, a pained look on her face.

"I didn't mean you, honey."

"Look, you all. I'll be right back."

Todd abruptly scooted Leslie out of the booth, race walking hurriedly towards back door.

"Todd!" exclaimed Leslie. "Where are you going?"

Everyone watched dumbfounded as Todd disappeared from the rear of the bar.

Billy asked, "Leslie, what's up with Todd. Is he...like, losing it?"

"I don't know for sure, but he's been taking a ton of drugs—pills and shit."

"Somebody ought to follow that dude," said Chris. "He could get in real trouble."

"I'll go!" cried Billy. "They don't call me Billy Saxon, ace detective for nothing!"

"Christ, Billy," said Dutch, "You couldn't find your sock inside your shoe."

"That's what you think!" declared Billy. "I'll give you a full report on our friend Todd—as soon as I get back!"

Leaving the Tavern, Billy was battered by a raging ice storm hurling gale force winds, tiny frozen daggers pelting his face. Visibility was poor, but he caught sight of Todd wandering aimlessly down a cobblestone path on the downtown mall towards University Boulevard. He crossed the street, heading for the Thomas Jefferson Rotunda. Billy thought he might be going to the library, but Todd kept moving towards a complex of dormitories bordering the lawns of the University campus. Todd passed several red brick buildings, then turned right, facing the front side of one of the larger dormitories. Walking parallel down a row of rooms fronted by identical brown wooden doors, he suddenly stood more erect, and began walking stiffly and formally, almost to the point of marching past each door, pausing every few steps as if he was a general inspecting the troops.

Caught off guard, Billy ducked behind a tree, but Todd seemed oblivious to his surroundings. Todd abruptly stopped and began staring blankly at a plate glass transparent dorm room in the middle of the row. After watching and shivering for a few minutes, Billy emerged from his hiding place, stealthily sneaking up behind Todd, and standing next to him, saying nothing.

"Do you think he wrote "The Gold Bug" at that desk?" asked Todd. "Gold Bug?"

"I think he died lost and drunk in Baltimore, didn't he?"

"Oh, yeah," said Billy. "Edgar Allen Poe. He went here, huh?"

"He felt a lingering pity and sorrow for the dead."

"Who? Poe? Christ, Todd, it's twenty degrees out here! Let's leave before we freeze our asses off!"

Todd giving the room a thousand-yard stare. "He knew the morbidity of it all...the deep dread of being...grim legions of suffering souls...dreary abyss, solitary eyes on fire..."

Billy took a hold of Todd's arm. "Let's get the fuck out of here!"

"Hideous drama...bloody red death...cerebral congestion..."

"That's enough!"

Billy grabbed Todd below the neck, yanking him back from the room, then tackling him like a linebacker. The two men tumbled down a sloping snowy hill, rolling together into a narrow ice-covered gully. Todd landed on his back with a dull thud and began laughing hysterically while gazing into the pitch black night, spreading his arms in an angel-in-the-snow position, oblivious to the icy stings peppering his face. A few feet away Billy lay on his side covered with snow, clutching his rib cage.

"Todd, are you okay?" asked Billy, struggling to get to his feet.

Todd was still mind-frozen in a hypnotic trance, muttering, "One more pitiless wave...one more final act of delirium...can't spend the night..."

The night wore on. Billy spent a couple hours calming Todd down, talking to him in a gentle soothing manner as if he was an injured child afraid to go to the doctor. Then, he walked him back to his car. Everyone had left the bar so Billy drove Todd to Leslie's apartment. As the two men entered, Todd took off his coat, tossed it on the floor, and trudged over to his recliner, a frantic Leslie rushing up to him. "Todd! Where have you been?"

Todd kept his eyes riveted to the TV's blank screen.

"You'll never guess where ole Todd was going," said Billy with strained cheerfulness.

"Where?" asked Leslie.

"Edgar Allen Poe's dorm room."

Leslie glared at Todd. "Why did you go there?"

"No reason," said Todd, "Except to ascend from the bottomless pit, venture to perdition."

"Come again, Todd?" said Billy.

155

Todd continued his rambling biblical, apocalyptic monologue. "Make the harlot desolate and naked...a sea of glass mingles with fire. Impurities of her fornication...beast must be slain...mighty angels will gore her flesh..."

"Todd," implored Leslie, "You're not making sense, and it's beginning to scare me. Billy, let's get him to a hospital. He's totally out of it."

Billy nodded. "I think you're right. Come on Todd, let's go for a ride."

"Where?"

"To a place that can help you," said Billy grabbing Todd by the coat sleeve. "You're sick and need help."

Todd yanked his arm from Billy's grip. "No, I don't. Don't be silly. I'm as healthy as Apostle John."

""I'm sure you are," said Billy. "But, let's just go and get a fast check up, okay?"

"Alright, but can I go to the bathroom first?"

"Of course."

In the bathroom, Todd gazed into the mirror checking out the O-Z-Z-Y tattoo on his four left-hand knuckles, fingering a golden cross dangling from his neck. An ephemeral, ghost-like figure loomed over his shoulder.

*"It's' about time you showed up. Don't worry, the judgments will be fair for those who shed the blood of Christian martyrs...make the harlot desolate and naked...into the lake of fire...scorching seals will deliver heat and cold... followed by inevitable locusts and poison winds. To Zion, then... long lost city of night...city of night---"*

"Hey Todd!"screamed Billy. "What are you doing in there?" Let's go!"

Moments later, Todd came out of the bathroom, the cross still dangling from his neck.

"Nice cross," said Billy. "New?"

"No," said Todd. "The saints carried them for ages."

"Right," said. Billy. "I'll get your coat. I'll drive."

"Where?"

"We're going to get you a check up, remember?"

"Weep no more. All things must pass."

"Todd," pleaded Leslie. "Listen to me! Billy and I are going to take you to the hospital so you can get some medical attention, okay?"

"Prostitute."

"What?" demanded Leslie.

"Todd," said Billy. "That's enough. Let's go."

Billy gripped Todd by the arm, pulled him out of the chair, straining mightily to haul him towards the door. Suddenly, Todd turned and drove his fist into Billy's face; Billy knocked out, falling hard, banging his head on the floor. Todd racing over to the fireplace, grabbing an andiron, and then manically charging towards Leslie who ran screaming into the bedroom, closing and locking the door seconds before Todd slammed into it. Pounding the door with an andiron, Todd bellowed, "You cannot escape the harlot's demise. Burn the fire! Burn the flesh---"

Billy pummeled Todd from behind with a ferocious tackle, sending them both crashing on top of the coffee table, shards of wood flying everywhere. Todd rolled over on top of Billy seizing the upper hand, pinning his arms to the floor. "You heathen! How dare you interfere with the divine Revelation!"

Todd forced his hands around Billy's throat, Billy gasping for air, choking, and rapidly turning blue. Billy struggled mightily to unleash Todd's grip, but soon he could feel the life being literally strangled out of him. Then, seconds before he was about to pass out, Leslie drove a steak knife into Todd's back.

Three months later, Leslie decided to see Todd once again. He was making little progress and the last two times she visited him he did not even recognize her. The doctor informed her that he would probably be hospitalized and taking anti-psychotic medications for the rest of his life. Todd was transferred to the Charlottesville Psychiatric Hospital following a two-month hospital stay to recover from his stab wounds. Leslie drove up the narrow paved road to the hospital, parked the car, and entered the building before riding the elevator to the third floor nurses' station. Shirley Albright, the nurse on duty, greeted her warmly.

"Why Leslie! Glad to see you!"

"Hi, Shirley. How are you doing?"

"Couldn't be better. My vacation coming up next week and I'm going to the Caribbean!"

"Terrific! Take me with you!"

"Oh," she said slyly, "I'm going with my new boyfriend."

"Well, I guess I'd certainly be in the way!"

Smiling, Shirley said, "I guess you want to see Todd."

"Is he okay?"

"Yes, he's alright. The same.. nothing ever changes around here."

Shirley led Leslie down the hall to Todd's room. "Wait here, Leslie. I'll get Fred."

Todd was no longer restrained all the time and he had not committed any more acts of violence since he attacked Billy. However, there was always an attendant present with any visitors. Fred arrived, escorting Leslie to Todd room.

Todd was sitting on the bed, his head completely shaved, smoking a cigarette.

"Hello, Todd," said Leslie.

"Hi, can I have a cigarette?"

"You're smoking one now."

"I mean for later. I'm almost out."

"I don't have any."

"Then why did you come?"

"I came to see *you*. How are you doing?"

"I'm okay."

"Do you know who I am?"

"Of course. Leslie Richards."

"You didn't know me the last time I was here."

"They changed my medication."

"And it's working?"

"Drowns out the voices. I was drooling all over myself..."

"Are you doing anything? Reading? Exercising?" "No, I can't read or write. Mostly, I just sit her wondering where my next cigarette is coming from."

"The guys are always asking about you. Billy told me to tell you hello."

"Billy's a good guy, but he keeps floating around somewhere...he could disappear."

"How could he disappear?"

"You know, like everyone else. He hasn't found anyone to talk to. He could dissolve and no one would ever know. Did you say you have some cigarettes?"

"No, I don't have any. I will bring you some next time."

"Those guys make me nervous."

"Who?"

"The guys in the band. I worry about them. I think they are around too many germs. Billy goes out with girls...too many germs...too much touching. You don't go out with boys, do you?"

"Sometimes."

"Too bad. Now, I have to worry about you."

"Catching germs?"

"You're better off alone."

"Todd."

"Yes?"

"I'm glad you're getting along here."

"Hey, I'm fine—Fred!"

Leslie had completely forgotten that Fred was in the room.

"What do you want Todd?"

"Yogurt. Blueberry yogurt. Tonight okay?"

"Sure, Todd. Blueberry it is."

"Todd, I have to go," said Leslie. "Please take care of yourself."

"Goodbye Leslie. Be careful. Remember, no touching!"

"Alright, Todd. No touching."

Leslie stood up, and walked towards the door. Before she left, she glanced back at Todd as he was staring off into space, smoking a cigarette, and blowing smoke rings into the air.

# Seat Open, Raise the Stakes

"Seat open!"
"Raise the stakes!"
"Quarter and a half?"
"Half and a bean!"
"Curtis pulled ass!"
"Motherfucker can't play no cards."
"Shut up and deal."

Four black men in the country club caddie shack were in the middle of a spirited game of knock rummy, shouting out a raucous chorus of opinions, expletives, and complaints reverberating within the corrugated tin walls of the makeshift holding pen for caddies.

Several other men and boys were playing the waiting game, talking among themselves, smoking cigarettes, drinking quarts of Colt 45 malt liquor, scanning the day's racing form, or listening for Griff, the caddie master to call their name. The caddies were a ragtag crew of working-class black men, white high-school dropouts, drifters and hobos, card sharks, petty thieves, drug dealers, horse racing gamblers, numbers runners, and marginally functioning alcoholics.

The day was sweltering, the humidity rising off the charts, and the shack providing no relief in the form of shade. It was so hot that a few of the men already decided they were not going out for a loop, even if Griff did call their name.

"I don't care if fuckin' Arnold Palmer himself shows up and asks for me personally," said caddie Clyde Roberts. "You ain't gettin' me out there today."

Hardly anyone noticed when a skinny freckle-faced young man with burnt-orange hair entered the shack, wearing clean, pressed khaki pants, a forest green polo shirt, and carrying a notepad and pencil. He looked more like a member's son than someone who would be interested in caddying. For a while he kept his distance from the caddies before drifting over to the card game. Dickie King had just plucked rummy in the blind, pissing off the other three players.

"Rummy dummies!" he screamed.

"Jesus Christ! You lucky bastard!" yelled Johnnie Johnson, slamming his cards into the pile.

"You believe that shit?" muttered Kapon. "A seven of diamonds—right in the gut!"

Bobby Stanford threw his cards down, grabbed his Colt 45 and took a huge gulp. "Hey, Kapon! Shut the fuck up! It's history—tell it to your history teacher! Deal the fuckin' cards."

2.   Kapon picked up the deck, shuffled the cards, and broke out in a song that sounded like a Motown hit:

> *Lady, lady, lady why do you holler?*
> *When nobody's seen your Johnny Dollar.*
> *I can't get no sleep... in this noisy street.*
> *I got to move... I got to find me a quiet place...*

"Okay, David Ruffin," said Johnnie Johnson, smiling as he lit a cigarette. "Keep dealing."

The other players picked up their cards as Kapon dealt seven to each one as they organized them according to suits.

"It's on you," said Johnnie, nodding to Bobby Stanford.

Bobby plucked a card from the deck, placed it in his hand, and then discarded the six of hearts.

"Don't you ever throw anything?" asked Dickie King, picking up the top card from the deck while discarding the three of spades.

The young man in the polo shirt stood over Dickie, eye-balling his cards.

Dickie turned around, hissing, "The fuck you looking at?"

"Sorry," said the young man, backing away and abruptly facing a white teenager with a pimply face wearing a silk-screened T-shirt bearing an image of a Stihl chainsaw.

"Excuse, me," said the young man, "Do you know anything about the incident at Mac's soda fountain four nights ago?"

The boy in the T-shirt shrugged, offering a blank look. "Huh?"

"The racial incident—"

"The fuck are you?" interrupted Bobby Stanford.

"I'm Jason Whittier. I'm a reporter for the *Beverly Banner*. I'm trying to do a story about what happened at Mac's—and Gene Washington's house."

Bobby tossed the queen of diamonds on the pile, then turned to the reporter. "Oh, we got a regular Clark Kent among us, fellas. He wants to know about those motherfuckin' white devils downtown."

"I want to cover both sides," said Jason. "Can you tell me what happened? I know Ritchie Edwards was involved, and I heard I could find him here."

"You mean Cush T.X.," said Johnnie Johnson.

"Cush T.X.? I thought he was Ritchie Ed—"

"Same thing," snapped Johnnie. "He changed his name. Where you been, boy?"

"I just moved to town a few months ago—from Indiana."

"And you wanna know about race relations in Beverly?" asked Kapon.

"Well," said Jason, "I know there was a fight at Mac's and Ritch—Cush T.X. and his friends were pretty upset—"

"Upset?" snarled Kapon, grabbing a card, then slamming it into the pile. "Would you be upset if you sat in a deserted restaurant for over a half-hour without being served? That ever happen to you, Mr. Polo Shirt?"

"No," said Jason. "But that's what I want to report. I want to know if Mac's is discriminating against black people."

"Son," said Johnnie, his voice dropping lower, "The whole damn country is discriminating. Why don't you print *that* in your little rag sheet?"

The kid with the Stihl T-shirt was listening intently to the conversation. "Hey, I heard about Mac's, but who the hell is Gene Washington?"

"Guess you don't know about the Set," muttered Dickie King.

"The Set?"

"Some white rednecks threw a bunch of rocks through his front window. Almost hit one of his girls."

"Why would they pick on Mr. Washington?"

"That don't concern you, Chainsaw," said Johnnie. "The man's house was terrorized because he was black."

At that moment, a brand new coffee-colored Cadillac pulled into the adjacent parking lot designated for visitors and caddies. A tall, well-built black man emerged from the car dressed in a resplendent Latin-style sky-blue suit, light burgundy shirt, and glistening white shoes with red laces. He sauntered slowly to the caddie shack carrying a small black leather case, dominating the space around him as if he was a movie star entering the Copacabana on Saturday night.

As he entered the open archway, several players and hangers-on took out slips of paper from their pockets, scribbling three-digit numbers while circulating a pencil. Cush T.X. unzipped his leather case, and collected the slips while writing in his notebook. He took a seat next to Kapon who began singing another verse:

> *Oh, there's a man upstairs with a radio,*
> *and he plays it all through the night.*
> *There's a couple in the apartment above my head,*
> *and all they do is... fuck and fight.*
> *I can't get no sleep in this noisy street...*
> *I got to move... I got to find me a quiet place...*

Cush T.X. pulled out a Kool cigarette, lighting it with a Zippo lighter, and inhaling deeply while listening to Kapon's smooth, velvety voice. "Kapon, you sound better than ever... cigarette?"

"Thanks, Cush."

"How the cards running?" asked Cush T.X., handing Kapon one of his Kools.

"Man, not so great. Fuckin' Hoyle couldn't win with these cards."

Bobby Stanford nodded to Cush T.X., then laid his open hand down on the bench. "Eighteen," said Bobby.

"Shit," muttered Kapon, tossing his cards on the discard pile.

"Beats me," said Dickie King. "I'm stuck with a million."

"I got thirteen," said Johnnie, showing Bobby his cards.

"Fuckin'-A!" cried Bobby, flipping his cards into the pile. "Sandbagged again!"

Each of the players handed Johnnie a dollar, except for Bobby who paid two dollars. Caddies were still drifting over to Cush T.X. to play their number for the day. One of them, Dolphe Simmons, asked him for a racing tip.

"I like Tango Red in the sixth at Garden State. He's got Kelso's bloodline in him, and he's dropping down in class."

"Good enough for me," said Dolphe.

All of a sudden Dickie King began singing totally off-key, imitating Kapon:

> *Oh, there's a man inside the caddie shack,*
> *and like Johnny Dollar, he knows how to sing.*
> *So let me tell you, brothers...*
> *In the land of the blind, the one-eyed-man is king,*
> *But in the caddie shack... Dickie's King!*

The caddies laughed uproariously, Kapon rushing over and gently jabbing Dickie with a few mock punches as if they were in a boxing match. "Kapon gonna float like a butterfly, and sting—the Dickie King!"

Dickie King grinned at Kapon, offered a couple of light jabs, then turned towards Cush T.X. "Kid thinks he's fuckin' Muhammad Ali, Cush."

"Come on, you jokers," said Johnnie Johnson. "Play some cards."

Jason had been standing by the entrance, waiting for a chance to talk to Cush T.X. He approached him like a nervous nephew needing to ask the Godfather for a favor. "Excuse, me, Mr. Cush T.X. I'm Jason Whittier from the *Beverly Banner*. Can I ask you a couple questions about the other day at Mac's soda fountain?"

Cush T.X. eyed the young man, then glanced over at the four card players. "This kid legit?"

"Seems to be," said Dickie, "Except for that polo shirt."

Cush T.X. smiled. "I didn't know they had reporters who looked like Howdy Doody," "Come here and sit down. What do you want to know?"

Jason took a seat on the bench.

"Smoke?"

"No thanks," said Jason. "I just want to know what happened at Mac's last Tuesday. I've heard conflicting stories, and I want to get it right."

"Conflicting stories, huh? Well, there's nothing conflicting about what happened—nothing conflicting at all. There's only one story, and that's the one where me and three of my friends went into Mac's and waited over half-an-hour to get waited on. Finally, my buddy Wilson went to the old lady who runs the place and asked her for some service. She said she was busy—she'd get around to it soon. Wilson told her that two tables had already been served ahead of us—"

"And what did she say?"

"She said, 'Oh, really? I wasn't aware of that.' Wilson told her she was full of shit and took a sugar container and dumped it on the counter. That's when five rednecks came over from two other tables and started giving Wilson a hard time, telling him to clean up the sugar. Then Wilson grabbed a napkin holder and bashed in one of these asshole's faces. Then all hell broke loose. There was like a bunch of us punching, swinging, and stomping all over the place—chairs flyin', dishes breaking over their hard heads, ashtrays flyin' in the air. Wilson threw one of those rednecks into the jukebox—cutting his ass, glass shattering all over the place. Well, someone must have called the cops, because three or four of them came in right in the middle of this melee—which those white boys were losing, by the way. The four of us turned around when the cops came in, and we thought, oh shit, more trouble—like getting clubbed over the head and taken to the joint. We were standing our ground waiting to see what they would do when one of the cops says, 'Ritchie, what the hell are you doing? You think you're the mayor or somebody?' Then I looked closer and it was Nate Green!"

"Nate Green?"

"A buddy of mine from Little League and high school—and by the way, he's black. I said to Nate, 'No, I'm just waiting to get served in this fine establishment, but I don't think they like us poor black folks very much. In fact, I am thinking about running for mayor and tar-and-feathering' these crackers out of town on a rail."

"And then what happened?" asked Jason.

"Well, the other cops started moving towards us with their clubs raised, but Nate raised up his arms like he was Moses parting the Red Sea, and told them cops to get the fuck out. Those white boys didn't know what to think. They were hovering in a corner shitting themselves, thinking Nate just might shoot their white asses. Nate as calm as a man holding four aces. He asked me and my buddies to step outside and told those white assholes to clean up the mess. We walked right past those other cops, who didn't know whether to shit or go blind. We strolled on down to the park bench by the bus stop, and Nate told us to just go on home and forget the whole thing. One of my buddies, Michael, asked if we were going to be arrested or anything. Nate said if anybody was going to be arrested it was that old racist fleabag of a woman and those white boys. Apparently it wasn't the first time people of color had a hard time getting served in that place. Nate said he was gonna find some reason to shut it down, or he was gonna bring in his whole family, pitch a tent, and just live there for a few weeks. That Nate is something else—hell of an athlete too."

"Did he shut it down?"

"Didn't have to. They changed their policy soon as they realized we would just keep comin' and comin' like we were marching with the Reverend King on the city of Washington, DC. There ain't no stopping us now."

"Can you tell me what happened at Gene Washington's house?"

"Not really. Everyone knows it was a couple of them white boys from Mac's. Don't know why they picked on Gene. They wouldn't have won a single damn football game in '52 if he wasn't on the team."

"Do you think it's over?"

"What's over?"

"You know—the racial tension."

"Son, it's just beginning."

# The Road Trip

Franklin Norris and Brittany Furman had it all planned. The weekend before Thanksgiving break they would take off and travel to Massanutten Ski Resort in Virginia where Franklin's parents owned a condominium. Franklin's dad had just bought him a new forest green Range Rover and he was dying to take a road trip. He was a gay theater major who acted in several plays with Brittany and one of the few male friends she had at the college. At the last minute Franklin asked Chad Overton to come along with them to share expenses. Franklin knew Chad was bi-sexual and hoped they would hook-up sometime during the trip. Chad was lukewarm to the idea, but accepted the invitation only because he was not particularly motivated in any other direction. He was going to New York City that weekend to be with his boyfriend James, a promising actor, but at the last minute James got a call from his agent asking him to fly to Los Angeles to audition for a TV pilot based on the "Friends concept."

On a chilly darkening afternoon, Franklin drove the Range Rover to the student union where Chad and Brittany were waiting outside. Chad tossed his backpack in the rear, jumping in the passenger seat with a cooler of beer while Brittany hopped in the backseat, dragging her suitcase behind her. They cruised steadily for a few miles approaching Interstate 66 before the lowering gray clouds suddenly burst open, pelting the highway with a heavy downpour. The heavy weekend traffic bottle-necked, and soon the threesome were snarled in a massive jam-up.

"Jesus Christ!" yelled Franklin, banging his fists on the steering wheel, "We might as well be stuck in an eight-hour delay at the airport!"

"Hey, chill," said Chad. "Let's get stoned."

"Right on," said Franklin.

"You got weed?" asked Brittany.

"Yeah, pretty good stuff."

Chad dug in his pocket producing a baggie of marijuana and some papers. He began rolling a joint. "I got this from my partner James. He's an actor living in L.A. right now. Pretty soon we're gonna move into a bungalow out there." Chad finished rolling the joint, passed it to Franklin who took a hit, then handed it back to Brittany.

"Good shit," said Franklin.

"I'll say," said Brittany, peering out the tinted window as the sloshing foggy line of stalled cars began moving along at a faster pace.

"This pot is far out," said Franklin.

"Looks like we're finally moving," said Brittany.

"Farm out?" asked Chad.

"What?"

"Never mind," muttered Chad.

"Hey, I forgot!" exclaimed Franklin. "I've got some Percocets!"

"Well, whip 'em out, fool!" cried Chad.

Brittany leaned forward, propping her arms on the back of the seats. "Hey, I could use a Percocet."

Franklin reached into his pants pocket, and grabbed a wad of rumpled aluminum foil. He handed it to Chad who unfolded it, revealing six pills.

"Might as well do them all," said Chad, offering two apiece to Franklin and Brittany while washing his down with a swig of Budweiser.

"Can I have a beer?" asked Brittany.

"Me too," said Franklin.

"Sure," said Chad, reaching into the cooler.

The traffic resumed a steady pace. The three travelers sat silently listening to REM's "Radio Free Europe"" blaring from the tape player. Just before dusk, the setting sun peaked through the clouds one last time, sending shimmering rays of light shooting through the Range Rover.

"Wow, look at the sun," said Franklin. "It's like we're heading for the Emerald City."

Then darkness descended on the road ahead, as a burnt-orange glow appeared on the dashboard. After a few miles Franklin said he had to go to the bathroom. Five minutes later he drove off the ramp, pulled into a Seven/Eleven and hustled out of the car. Chad went inside to get another twelve-pack. Brittany stayed in the car half-asleep. When Chad came out of the store, he walked over to Franklin who was filling up the tank.

"Do you want me to drive?" asked Chad.

"Sure," said Franklin.

Franklin finished refueling, and then hopped in the passenger seat. Chad took over the wheel, easing the car out of the parking area onto the highway. He immediately ejected REM's album *Murmur* in favor of George Thorogood's *Maverick*.

"It's time for some *real* rock 'n roll," asserted Chad, as a sonic blast of electric guitars and saxophone shattered the silence, giving way to Thorogood shouting, *"I drink alone—with nobody else!"*

"That's more like it," screamed Franklin, slapping the dashboard with both hands as if it was a drum set, singing loudly, "Yeah, I drink alone, motherfucker!"

Chad joined in the chorus, "Yeah, I got my good buddy-Weiser and my pal Jim Beam!"

Brittany energetically joined in, swaying back and forth to the beat as the threesome partied down the open highway totally stoned, feeling gloriously happy and free.

After cruising for twenty miles, Chad changed the tape to Phil Collins and set the cruise control to 70 miles an hour. He glanced back, noticing Brittany's shadowy figure sprawled across the seat, a dreamy look on her face. Her shoulders were pressed together making her breasts seem larger in her low-cut tank-top. Chad felt his penis swelling between his legs. He peered over at Franklin, shaking him, "Hey! Wake up! Get me a beer, okay?"

"Sure," said Franklin, lifting out a Budweiser out of the cooler and handing it to Chad. As he leaned forward, Franklin stared down at Chad's penis before slowly lifting his eyes. Chad smiled thinly, nodding. Franklin leaned down, stretching his left arm awkwardly around Chad's waist. Chad unzipped his pants. Franklin eased his mouth on Chad's penis, gently cupping his right hand around it. Stroking it smoothly, he licked the tip like an ice cream cone, sucking harder and harder, steadily pumping up and down. Chad's body vibrated spasmodically as he fought to repress moaning sounds stifled inside his compressed lips. Gripping the steering wheel like a crossbar on a roller coaster, Chad raised his hips, slamming his head back into the seat before ejaculating in Franklin's mouth. Franklin swallowed the semen, then drew away, exhausted.

Smiling to herself in the back seat, Brittany loved every minute of it.

A half-hour later, Chad announced, "We just came to Interstate 81. It won't be too much longer."

Brittany pretended to wake up. "How's the weed situation?"

"We smoked it all," said Franklin.

Brittany sat up, stretching her arms and rubbing her neck. "Well then, it's a good thing I have some Ecstasy, huh?"

"Ecstasy!" shouted Franklin. "Far out! Let's do it right now! How much do you have?"

"I think I got six or seven left. Let me see." Brittany rummaged through her pocketbook, took out a small change purse, and unzipped it. "I have six. How convenient! Two apiece should fuck us up pretty good."

"I'll say," agreed Chad.

Brittany gave Chad and Franklin two hits apiece, and then asked, "How about a beer to wash these down?"

Franklin dug up a beer and snapped the tab, handing it to Brittany who immediately gulped down her pills.

Chad continued cruising down the highway, unknowingly slowing down to 55 miles an hour. He blinked his eyes as oncoming cars whizzed past him like a cluster of motorized comets flaring psychedelic spears of light.

"Hey guys," said Chad, "Let's take a break. I'm beginning to see double and triple."

"Good," said Brittany. "I need to pee."

Chad drove a few more miles searching for an exit ramp. He turned off an exit for the town of Mt. Jackson, veering to the right down a dark isolated country road. He drove about a mile, then turned right into a vacant lot, easing the Range Rover behind a tree, out of sight of the road.

Chad shut off the SUV, lowering his head on the steering wheel, sighing deeply.

"Nice job," said Franklin. "I don't know how you did it. I'm too fucked up to walk, much less drive."

"Let's hang here for a little bit," said Chad. "We're in no hurry."

The threesome got out of the SUV. Chad and Franklin walked over to a clump of trees and sat down in the grass. Brittany disappeared behind a row of tall bushes. She came back minutes later shivering from the cold, rubbing her shoulders.

"Hey guys, it's getting colder. Let's hang out in the Rover."

"Good idea," said Franklin. "The seats fold down."

The three travelers returned to the vehicle. Franklin twisted a couple small knobs, adjusting the seats to a flat sitting area. Chad and Brittany jumped in the back. Franklin went up front, started the car, turned on the heat, and fetched a bottle of Deer Park water from his backpack. When he returned to the back of the vehicle they formed a circle, sitting silently while passing the bottle back and forth. High on weed, Percocets and Ecstasy, the drugs were beginning to form a strong camaraderie among the three passengers. Chad reached up front and slipped in a tape of *Marvin Gaye's Greatest Hits*. Brittany moved closer to Franklin, put her arms around him and gave him a big wet kiss. Franklin leaned over and kissed Brittany, beads of sweat forming on his brow. As the song "Let's Get It On" wafted out of the tape deck, Franklin moved his hands around Brittany's breasts, massaging them gently. Brittany removed her tank top and unhooked her bra. She took Franklin's hand, guiding it slowly between her thighs, and then slipped off her mini-skirt and panties.

Chad sat mesmerized as Brittany leaned back, splaying out her legs. Franklin removed his pants and mounted her, his ass arching closer to Chad's face. Chad quickly removed his clothes, crawled around and kissed Franklin on the mouth. Brittany wiggled out from underneath Franklin, searching for Chad's penis. She sucked him off while Franklin rolled over in back of Brittany forcing his middle finger up her ass. Chad eased his penis out of Brittany's mouth and went behind Franklin, jamming his penis into him. Brittany watched Chad fuck Franklin, then inched over and separated the two of them, making them lie down side-by-side. She put Franklin's penis in her mouth, sucked on it, then guided it towards Chad who sucked it vigorously. Chad left Franklin and began fucking Brittany while Franklin watched, masturbating. Franklin came; Chad ejaculated into Brittany. Then, the three exhausted bodies collapsed in a sweaty heap, laboring to breathe, sighing deeply, wiped out.

Brittany sat up. She found the water bottle on the floor and took a sip before passing it to Chad who had rolled over beside her. From the corner, Franklin crawled on his hands and knees, and leaned up against the side door. Chad handed him the water bottle. As the physical rushes subsided, Chad and Franklin lapsed into an uncomfortable silence. But, Jody was still tingling with erotic rushes, bathing in the mellow love power of Ecstasy. Grooving to the sensual beat of "Sexual Healing," her head swayed gently, soaking in the soothing warmth of two male bodies, enthralled with the strong emotional binding power of romantic, sensual love.

"Hey guys," said Brittany. "I want you to know I really like both of you a lot. I am really glad I made this trip. I mean, I had no idea we were going to, you know...do all this! But, I'm glad we did and I *really* care about both of you."

Chad and Franklin nodded. Franklin said, "I hope this doesn't mess up the rest of the trip. I want to be friends."

"Is this X the bomb, or what?" added Chad. "Yes, we should definitely be good friends."

Brittany was feeling more love for these two individuals than anyone in her whole life. Sitting quietly in the shadowy darkness of the night, she was overwhelmed by a rare encounter with what she believed was true intimacy. Without considering the consequences, Brittany abruptly made her confession: "I'm HIV positive."

"What!" screamed Chad.

"You're what!" yelled Franklin.

Breaking into sobs, Brittany fumbled for a Kleenex in her pocketbook.

"Jesus, fucking Christ! You fucking lunatic!" screamed Chad. "Are you for real?"

"I'm sorry," moaned Brittany. "I just couldn't live with myself if I didn't tell you guys. I love you *so much.*"

"Well," cried Chad, hovering over Brittany. "You got a *hell* of a way to show it! I'm gonna kill you—you psycho bitch!"

Teeth clenched and fists raised, Chad lunged towards Jody, knocking her to the floor, punching her in the stomach, and then reached down, grabbed her by the neck, squeezing the life out of her.

Franklin charged, tackling Chad, screaming "You're going to kill her!" Chad screaming right back, "Damn right, I am! She gave us AIDS!"

Franklin yanked Chad's hands apart, forcing him to release his grip, leaving Brittany lying on the floor choking and gasping for breath.

Enraged, Chad bellowed, "She's a piece of shit!" She deserves to die!" He seized his backpack from the rear of the SUV, viciously swung the door open and stormed up front to get his cooler. Banging the door shut, he ran as if possessed by demons 234down the country road towards the highway.

"God, I thought he was going to kill me," said Brittany.

"Are you okay?"

"I think so. My head hurts."

"Do you need a doctor?"

"No. I'll be all right. I guess that puts an end to the trip," "I'm afraid so," said Franklin.

Following an awkward pause, Franklin asked, "Are you really HIV-positive?"

"I don't know," said Brittany.

Printed in the United States
By Bookmasters